Lock Down Publications and Ca$h Presents

BLOOD AND MAYHEM

Living In My Empire

Written By

JJ DORSEY

First Edition 2025

Printed in the United States of America

Lock Down Publications
P.O. Box 944
Stockbridge, GA 30281
www.lockdownpublications.com

Like our page on Facebook: Lock Down Publications
www.facebook.com/lockdownpublications.ldp

Stay Connected with Us!

Text **LOCKDOWN** to 22828 to stay up-to-date with new releases, sneak peaks, contests and more…

Like our page on Facebook:
Lock Down Publications

Join Lock Down Publications/The New Era Reading Group

Visit our website:
www.lockdownpublications.com

Follow us on Instagram:
Lock Down Publications

Email Us: We want to hear from you!

Dedication

Love to all my people – love, truth, peace, freedom, and justice to all my bros. I'll be home shortly. I mean it this time. I done lost a lot of people since I've been down, but I ain't shed a single tear, just waiting to get home to my family. One thing I know for certain is that I ain't coming back. No, sir. I won't even jaywalk. Hahahahaha. Shout out to Ca$h and everybody at Lockdown Publications. From the authors to the people behind the scenes who help keep this show on the road, I'm forever grateful. I hope whoever reads this last installment in *The Real Baddies* trilogy thoroughly enjoys the ride. I did my best to detail the story just as I envisioned it. I'll likely need an adult film star to film some of these scenes once the movie comes, lol, and maybe Stephen Spielberg to assist me in directing the rest, but in the words of Kitty Jae, "It'll be a blockbuster." Share my books with a friend. Much love and gratitude to you, the reader.

Add me on Facebook, follow me on Instagram.
Facebook: Author Rio and Author King-Rio
Instagram: @authorrio5 Undying Love.

Table of Content

Chapter 1

The summer night air had a cool but radiant breeze in the city of Detroit with the streets of downtown teetering with a variety of people on a perfect Friday. The night clubs and restaurants were bustling and on stop mode tonight. But the bars were the hot spots with its vibrant décor in real woodwork, and warm earth tones to match the flow of the dimly lit fluorescent lightning set a calm, sensual mode. The music was low and hummed a soft sound of jazz, as the scene of people were active and turnt.

Lacey strutted into the place, dressed in a tight, tan, fitted, Gucci dress that stopped just above her knees, exposing her thick thighs and lily tattoos. She wore two gold Cuban link chains, both slightly different in length to complement her dress, her features, as well as her attitude, showing enough cleavage to make the room feel high off of sex and seduction. She was accompanied by a younger female when she ran into a familiar face waiting for her at the bar, ordering Hennessy on the rocks with a touch of Red Bull.

He was a man of business, and bred in the slums, so the savage in him made him a vicious nigga by heart and a rich one too. His jewelry, from neck to wrist, danced with canary yellow crushed diamonds like a disco ball. He wore a black Louis Vuitton suit, Red Bottom Louis loafers, and appeared to be by himself for the moment — bodyguardsnot too far away.

"Hold on," Lacey told her friend. "I wanna talk to dis nigga alone." The female nodded and disappeared outside.

Dominic looked out the corner of his eyes to see Lacey walking in his direction. She looked gorgeous, but the sight of him didn't change her demeanor or the hard stare and distasteful feelings Lacey had for him now. Things between them had taken a turn for the unexpected. Their love for each other no longer existed; their passion for loving each other was torn.

"You look amazing as always, Lacey."

"Yeah, thank you, and so do you, Dominic."

"Sit down. I need to talk to you." Dominic gestured to the vacant seat next to him.

Lacey, her blood boiling, took a seat next to her ex-fiancé. With a Glock 10 in her purse and her homegirls outside, ready for whatever, it was obvious she didn't trust him at all. The energy between the two spoke for itself.

"So, what's up? What you sippin' on tonight?"

"I'm not thirsty. You know what's up, and why we meeting here? You left me to rot, Dominic."

"Look, sweetheart, let me clarity something between us two. I searched for you, tore the streets up trying to find you, and when I couldn't, I just thought you packed up and just disappeared on me after your birthday for a while. I got in contact with some of my people to see if you reached out to anyone we knew to find you. But when they tapped into the streets, word got out about some niggas snatching you up. I rounded up every hitta to get you back, but it was too late."

"Nigga, do you think for once I'ma sit up here and listen to this lame ass shit?"

"First of all, you can believe whatever the fuck you want to believe, and honestly, I don't care if you don't. But I'm telling you what it is doe."

"Nigga, you had me replaced like yesterday, like I never existed in the first place, and when I was snatched up, you had the audacity to buy your new bitch a condo in Los Angeles and provide for all her financial stability and needs.

Is that how you do a woman you're engaged to marry? By fucking on me with a new bitch? And while I was missing?"

"You better watch your muthafucking mouth. I did love you, Lacey."

"Look, fuck all that. I came here for one thing and one thing only. Where's Madame Charity?"

"So, that's how you coming at me now?"

"Nigga, you know I'm a bitch about my business. Before I met you, I was the same. You know what's up and how I'm bumming. So, stop wit' all dat rah rah shit or we gone have problems."

"Aight, you got it. The package outside locked up real tight."

"How did you find that bitch?"

"Like I told you before, I got my connections and resources. Just like how I found out about the kidnapping and the news about your best friend."

"Why you doing this for me? What is your goals and motives? And to add, my best friend's death should've been on the news. They left her for dead in the streets."

"There is none. I just want you to know that there is no hard feelings between us, Lacey. And I'm sorry about Carmela."

Dominic stood up, and Lacey did the same. Arm in arm, they made their exit from the bar and walked onto the summer streets of Detroit. It was getting late, so all the activity and traffic had died down a lot. The only movement came from inside the bar they'd just walked out of with the exception of a few passing cars and open restaurants.

When Lacey's Red Bottoms hit the hard pavement, she took in her surroundings, on the lookout for anything suspicious and out of the ordinary. Dominic still could not be trusted in her eyes, so she had to keep one eye on him too.

"Where is she?" Lacey asked curiously. Dominic nodded to his matte grey Bentley, keys in hand. He hit the alarm button and unlocked the car doors.

Lacey could sense something was off. She proceeded to follow Dominic to his car with caution, but then, she stopped.

"What's up? You want her or what?" Dominic turned and asked.

Lacey could clearly see that something didn't add up. It was too sudden and funny how things just seemed too easy. "Naw, I'm cool," Lacey uttered.

"What the fuck you mean, 'naw, you cool?' You think I wasted my time and went out my way for you jus' so you could back out? Fuck naw. You wanted her. You got her," he said coldly.

"First off, you never told me how you found her, Dominic, and I'm still trying to figure out how. You never once mentioned that shit."

"I told your ass I got connections and resources," Dominic replied angrily.

"What fuckin' connections and resources, Dominic? Theo or Neisha couldn't find Madame Charity, but I'm supposed to believe that you, of all people, were the one to find her?"

Dominic took a step closer to Lacey, and they locked eyes. Lacey could see the rage in Dominic's eyes.

And then, Lacey felt a dark presence looming about. She recognized some of the faces of Dominic's hittas creeping out of the alleyway like shadows birthed from darkness. It was a setup.

Lacey swiftly took the pistol from her purse and fired off a few shots to send Dominic and his crew ducking for cover. She took cover behind a parked car but not before hearing shots being fired back at her and feeling a bullet rip through her upper left arm. She fell against the side of the car, cringing from the pain.

Dominic and his crew continued to spray bullets in Lacey's direction to try and keep her pinned down. But little did he know that she had prepared for this.

Lacey's homegirls, Tonya and Angelica, and Dee-Dee, who escorted Lacey into the bar, got out of a white Jaguar truck and opened fire while making their way to her side. Seconds later, a maroon-colored Lincoln truck screeched around the corner, sped up the street in their direction, and came to a halt. The doors flew open, and machine gunfire from AK-47s and Mack 11s hit the night skies.

Tat! Tat! Tat! Tat! Tat! Tat! Tat! Tat!

The barrage of gunfire shot out car windows and shattered glass windows of restaurants, shops, and storefronts, violently cutting down a couple of Dominic's men and sending innocent bystanders lounging in the bar scattering for cover. It sounded like a world war had broken out in the downtown streets of Detroit with the night of chaos and screams filling the air.

Dominic opened fire on the Lincoln truck with his Glock 9 that he brandished as he stood, poised, behind a parked vehicle. With the gun in his hand and his arm outstretched, he put his attention on Lacey, trying to line her up. His expression showed that he was enraged and blood thirsty.

"You stupid ass bitch," he screamed.

Lacey's backup quickly applied more pressure to Dominic and his crew and gained the upper hand. Dominic and his men were outnumbered. He stumbled back, still firing at the threat. The men in the truck were treacherous and trying to kill any and everything in their line of fire. They made the streets look like the streets in Afghanistan. It was as if two military groups were at war with each other.

Dominic started to retreat to his car with bullets whizzing by his head, and before he could get into his car, shots tore through the flesh of his right shoulder and left thigh. He quickly threw himself into the driver's seat of the Bentley, slamming the door behind him, as he sped away as quickly as he could, while his Bentley was being riddled by bullets.

Tonya and Angelica helped Lacey from the side of the car and carried to the Jag truck. Her dress sleeve and down the side of her dress were coated in blood. The pain was agonizing.

"That bitch ass nigga," Lacey yelled, as the Jag truck peeled away with her in the back.

Police sirens could be heard getting closer in the distance. In the aftermath of the shootout, nine bodies laid dead, soulless.

Chapter 2

The scorching Ypsilanti, Michigan sun seemed intense, as it seeped through the windshield of Joveezy's cheery red G-wagon. The Southside was active, as the city began to wake up.

With his sound system bumping hard, truck filled with Kush smoke, and the air conditioner on blast, Joveezy was in his element. Ypsilanti was his playground, and he was living like a true king, taking the reins of the streets little by little, piece by piece, and building a legacy. He had all that a man could want – money, power, respect – and the women were just an added bonus.

He was building an empire with his righthand, Ced, by his side every step of the way. And with a killer plug, he was game tight. He was climbing the ranks of the underworld where most men respected his name, and some feared him. He ruled the streets with a fierce heart. He was smart, deadly, and goal oriented.

Ypsilanti had a lot to offer, and Joveezy was able to afford anything and go anywhere he pleased with no hesitation or problems. With the connections he had, he was being introduced to new plugs and gaining new territory from the Midwest down to the south.

Joveezy drove his G-Wagon toward Ann Arbor to Crystal Creek Drive. The houses that lined the block were million-dollar houses. He parked in the driveway of a beige, brick house with a two-car garage and stepped out into the beating sun.

He walked up to the door and knocked twice and then three more times after that. No one answered, so he checked for the spare key in the flowerpot by the door. When he found it buried in the dirt, he unlocked the door and entered the house.

Polished wood decorated the hallway floor leading to the living room. A large-screen television was mounted to the wall. Connected to the living room, there was a dining room and a kitchen. Up the hall were two bedrooms with a bathroom in each with a clear standing shower cabin along with a built in jacuzzi tub nestled in its own private nook. Scented candles and oil fragrance filled the whole house with candy apple and lavender.

"What's up, gorgeous?" he asked with a smile.

Lisa looked up from watering her plants and smiled. "Hi, Daddy. I missed you," she said, approaching Joveezy.

The two embraced and passionately kissed. They had known each other since high school and had been best friends and lovers ever since. Lisa was his rock. She was intelligent and great with handling finances. She was his ride or die and a very loyal bitch who could tame and keep him on his toes.

Joveezy knew he had a down-to-earth bitch. She never asked for anything, but she needed not to because she was rolling in money from her parents' twenty-three-million-dollar inheritance, which helped Joveezy out. From the first time they laid eyes on each other, he knew he had to have her at any cost. She was beautiful, and her looks could have landed her in the modeling industry as a thick and curvy vixen.

Lisa wanted him to lock her down. She was his possessive pleasure, his passionate playmate, and she was off limits to anyone who thought about having her. Lisa was obsessed with Joveezy, and she let that be known to any female when they were out in public together.

"Damn! I can never keep my eyes and hands off of you when we're together," Joveezy said with lust in his eyes.

"You like what you see, Daddy?" Lisa asked seductively.

"I love everything I see. Now take it off."

"My pleasure, Daddy," Lisa said with a little moan in her voice.

Lisa slowly began to peel her dress away from her flesh, wiggling her fat, juicy ass from out of the material and letting the dress fall to the floor, revealing that she wasn't wearing anything underneath.

Joveezy grabbed her and wrapped his arms around her waist. Lisa's naked body was soft and smooth against his, and her nipples were hard against his chest. Her booty was soft and juicy, and her pussy was freshly shaved to his liking.

"I want you so bad right now," Joveezy proclaimed.

Lisa responded by sticking her hands in his pants and stroking his dick.

Joveezy took a step back, took off his white, V-neck t-shirt, kicked off his wheat Timberland boots and tan True Religion jeans until he was left in nothing but his socks and Calvin Klein briefs. His hands proceeded to roam freely over Lisa's curves, caressing her slim waist and fat, jiggling booty. As he continued to caress and kiss all over Lisa's body, his dick grew harder and harder in his briefs as if threatening to break loose from its restraints.

Lisa could feel the large bulge poking at her nakedness, begging for attention. The two kissed hungrily, their tongues wrestling with each other's. Joveezy cupped Lisa's large breasts, squeezed them, and sucked on her hard nipples.

Lisa moaned out, "Ooh, shit, Daddy. I want you to fuck the soul out of me right here, right now. Please, Daddy," she said seductively.

Joveezy loved Lisa's bold, freaky side. He removed his briefs, exposing his thick, lengthy, hard dick to her. He began to stroke himself slowly, never taking his eyes off of her. At the sight of this, Lisa sat on the antique wine table and began to play with herself. As she fingered herself, her moaning began to grow intense while watching Joveezy stroke himself.

"Come give Daddy that tongue and throat," he said.

Lisa got off the table and dropped down to her knees in front of him, gripping his dick in her small hand. She leaned forward and licked the mushroom head of his dick before taking the tip into her mouth then sliding her wet lips and tongue farther down his dick. She deep throated and gagged on him down to the base and back to the tip, sucking while looking up at him with blissful eyes.

He started to moan, as he gripped the back of her head and slowly started to thrust his hips. Tears began to roll down her face, as her saliva dripped from his dick and the corner of her mouth onto the patio floor.

"Ooh, fuck! Right there! Yeah, fuck, suck that dick," he grunted through clenched teeth.

Lisa's slurping sounds grew louder. Joveezy looked down into her eyes, loving what she was doing to him. His dick was wet with saliva, and he could feel the pressure building up and rushing to the tip of his dick, causing it to jerk, and then the strong suction from Lisa's lips made him explode into her mouth.

Lisa sucked up every drop of his cum and swallowed with no hesitation. She stroked his dick while still sucking him dry to make sure she didn't miss any trickles of cum.

He quickly pulled out of her clenching jaws.

Lisa looked up at him, licking her lips, her eyes filled with hunger and lust. She got off her knees, and Joveezy positioned her doggy style over the antique wine table. She gripped the sides of the table and spread her legs, giving Joveezy access to her goods. She could feel her juices running down her inner thighs.

Joveezy grabbed her waist and slowly penetrated her inch by inch, feeding her as much as she was allowing him, until he hit bottom.

Lisa moaned, "Uh-uh, shiiitt, Daddy."

Joveezy began to thrust at a steady pace. Slapping her jiggling booty, he wrapped his fist around her curly hair, pulling her head back far enough to lightly choke her. Lisa loved every minute of it.

As he slid in and out of her, Lisa matched him with each thrust. A light breeze passed through the mesh screen of the windows, blowing on her already hard nipples, as their sexual endeavor played out on the back patio. Lisa's pussy throbbed nonstop around his dick as if her love box was deep throating him to no end.

"Fuck, Daddy," she cried out. "You doing that shit just right. Fuck me just like that. Don't stop hitting that spot! Uh, shit. Uh-uh-uh-aw. Yeah, Daddy, that dick feels so good in me!"

"Fuck, yeah. Shiit, this pussy wetter than a muthafucka. Cum all on dis dick for Daddy," Joveezy said, feeding Lisa his dick all the way to her core.

Joveezy felt his balls start to contract, and pressure was starting to build up, threatening to release his seed deep inside her. Her pussy was gushy and beyond good. It was fantastic, and it was making him go crazy, giving her all back shots like he was doing. His breath came heavier and heavier, as he pounded in and out of Lisa, unable to pull out before busting a load because Lisa's warm, wet pussy and suctioning were not letting him resist or be released from its resting place.

He kept fucking her, blowing her back out with long, hard strokes, becoming a passionate savage in her tight, wet pussy. His dick started to jerk uncontrollably, as he released his warm semen deep into her, gripping her hips for stability as he came a second time.

Both of them were exhausted, as they tried to catch their breath from the orgasm that had rocked them.

"Damn, Daddy, I love it when you put it on me like that," Lisa said, still trying to control her breathing.

"You love when I put that work in, baby?"

"Hell yeah, Daddy. I love it when you dig deep in me like that. Me and my pussy be going crazy," she said.

They gathered their clothing and headed to the bedroom where they wrapped around each other in bed and continued fucking again and again until the night skies claimed its share in the world.

***

Joveezy laid back on the bed, deep in thought, while Lisa laid on his chest with her eyes closed.

"I need to handle some moves, baby. The money ain't gone make itself."

Lisa smacked her lips. "You know money ain't never a problem with us, so cut it out."

"What you mean? You know I got a make sure business is running how it's supposed to. So, why you tripping?"

Lisa smacked her lips again. "I ain't tripping, bae, but I want my time with you for at least three days."

"Aight," Joveezy said without protest. "I got you, Ma."

Lisa looked him in the eyes as if ready to continue to protest but decided against it. Instead, she gave him a soft kiss on the lips.

"I'm a go hop in the shower and put on something casual. I'm leaving you my Mercedes truck and driving the Hellcat for the rest of the night."

"Alright, bae," said Lisa. "Make sure you go get everything you need out of it before you leave."

"I will, but while I'm in the shower, can you set out a fit for me? I have a meeting that I need to attend to."

"I got you, Daddy."

He got out of the bed and entered the bathroom, cutting on the faucet to the sink first. Joveezy stared into the double-sided mirror mounted above the gold side-by-side sinks. The countertop was a polished white marble. Looking back at himself, he thought about the upcoming events with Ced. They'd put a nice lick together and had been surveilling and casing out their target for some time now. All Joveezy could think about was the goldmine they could possibly obtain, and he was itching for some action.

Joveezy cut the water off to the sink and cut the shower on and took a shower. Thirty minutes later, he stepped out the shower to dry off, brush his teeth, and groom up before heading back into the bedroom.

When he entered the room, Lisa was nowhere in sight. On the bed, laid out for him, was a black Ferragamo suit, a red button up with a red necktie to match, Guess Mist cologne, and a Glock 9mm.

Joveezy smiled to himself. "That's why I fucks with this bitch because baby love me till death," he said to himself.

After he got dressed, he went to his dresser drawer and pulled out a gold choker with white and gold diamonds, a gold Cuban link chain, and a shoulder holster for his Glock. As he put on his accessories, his cell phone began to ring. He checked the screen to see who it was before answering.

'What's brakking, Slime?" he answered.

"Ain't nothing to it, just booling. Let's link up at the spot out in Liberty Square, so we can put this demo in motion."

"Aight, Ru. I'ma spin on you in'a minute," said Joveezy.

"Bet dat up, P-funk," Ced said before the call ended.

Joveezy left the bedroom in search of Lisa. He found her in the kitchen refrigerator, bent over with nothing on but a t-shirt. He smacked her booty and watched it jiggle. She yelped, rubbing her butt.

"I'm bout to go handle business, sweetheart," he said, as he gave her a kiss on her soft lips.

"Okay, Daddy. I love you and be safe."

"I will try my best, but you know how shit goes."

Joveezy took the keys to the Mercedes, hitting the alarm and unlocking it, before replacing them with the keys to the Hellcat Charger. He went outside to the truck and hit the button to the garage where he'd retrieved a grey on black Charger. Before leaving, he grabbed two Adidas gym bags out of the backseat of the truck and placed them in the trunk of the Charger. He closed the trunk, and as he drove away from the house, he called Lisa to tell her the truck was all hers and proceeded to his next destination.

Chapter 3

The spot in Liberty Square was a townhouse set up similar in style and looks to the others, brown brick structures with white shelling. The two-story house was a drop off location for Joveezy and his crew. Security cameras were mounted outside as well as inside, watching the premise from every angle, including the streets in both directions. Two American bullies patrolled the outside perimeter, while a cane corso roomed the inside of the house as extra security against intruders and burglars.

Joveezy parked in front of the townhouse and exited the vehicle. He popped the trunk of the Charger and retrieved the two Adidas gym bags before heading into the house. In the living room, the air was thick with Kush smoke. Four of Joveezy's front runners, Rawdy, Banks, Vic, and Lil Loko, were sitting on the couch, playing GTA on the Xbox One. Upon his presence, they looked up and greeted him. On the table, laid out, was a kilo and a half of cocaine, a pint of Raspberry Kush, small vials of crack, and a SO9 and an AR pistol.

In the dining room was a round table with eight women in nothing but their panties, counting stacks of money through a money machine. Overlooking them were armed men with micro-Uzis.

Joveezy took the first duffle bag and emptied its contents out onto the table. Stacks of money spilled out on the table, and the women proceeded to feed it through the money counter.

Joveezy headed upstairs to the second floor with the other duffle bag. The first stacks room contained monitors that showed the video feed of everything the eye could see and was being watched by two of his used secret detail. He headed past the surveillance room and went up the hall to a back room and opened the door.

The room was painted red, and portraits of models hung up on the wall. Two stripper poles stood from floor to ceiling in front of a long black couch. On the far side of the room, a small bar with bar stools decorated the back room, and a ninety-inch, flat screen, smart TV hung up on the wall. It showed ESPN 1 and 2 and the local news.

Ced sat at the bar, talking on his cell phone, as Joveezy walked up.

"I'm a hit you back up later, Shay. Kiss my baby for me and tell her I said Daddy loves her and good night," Ced said before hanging up the phone.

Joveezy stepped behind the bar and poured himself a glass of Don Julio. "So, what's brackin' on that demonstration, Blood?" he asked Ced.

"Word is that shipment is supposed to be rolling in at the abandoned warehouse in Detroit at one in the morning. The shipment contains crates of goods from guns to drugs, money, etc. The warehouse also contains a safe locked in the office."

"So, how many niggas is going to be present? And do we got shit set in motion to hit these niggas the right way?"

"Yeah," said Ced. "We tryna slide tonight because that is when they are supposed to be unloading. After that, they gonna move the shipment quick to the next location."

"What about surveillance?" asked Joveezy.

"Security is tight, but not as tight as it should be. I'm guessing they don't want to draw too much attention, especially at an odd time of the night. So, outside security can be handled. It's just the matter of once getting inside, what type of consequences we gone face. Other than that, we golden."

Joveezy took a sip before asking his next question. "So, how many hittas do we got for the job?"

"We got six hittas and two drivers."

"Aight," he said, as he placed the second duffle bag on the bar counter. "In the meantime, I got twenty kilos of soft right here. I'ma need you to send these to the spot in the greens."

"I will have Spunk come pick these up tomorrow and drop them off," Ced responded.

Joveezy looked at his watch. It was 10:30 p.m. He took another sip from his glass and told Ced to have everyone ready in thirty minutes and to meet him in the basement.

Done with his meeting with Ced, Joveezy left the room and headed downstairs to the basement. The basement was fully furnished. Beige carpet covered every corner on the floor with furniture, and there was a full kitchen, a small library, a game room, and a conference room decorated with a twenty seat, mahogany, gold trimmed table, a large plasma screen television, and a large portrait of angels and demons battling mounted on the wall. The portrait hung up on the wall from floor to ceiling. There was a door a few feet away.

Joveezy took a set of keys from his pocket to unlock the door. He stepped into the room, as the light automatically came on upon his presence.

The room was a panic room converted into an office. The walls were made of three-inch titanium steel that was covered with insulated padding to keep the room at a steady and warm temperature with wooden wall panels to touch it up. It was decorated with a futon, a desk, laptop, a large flat screen that showed the security camera feed, and a tall safe was in the corner of the back room.

He went to the safe and entered a four-digit pin code, and the safe popped open. Inside were a few handguns, a SD9-VE with a thirty-two round clip and fifty round drums. There was a Glock 45, a .44 Magnum, two rifles, an AK-47with a hundred round drum, and a M14. There was also $500,000, four bulletproof vests, drugs, and a manilla envelope.

Joveezy grabbed the envelope and closed the safe. He exited the office, locked it up, and then went to the conference table to take his place at the head of the table, while he waited for Ced and his soldiers, so they could go over the details of executing their mission.

Ced, along with Rawdy, Banks, Vic, Lil Loko, and four of Ced's handpicked hittas, showed up on the dime. All of them were dressed in black and ready to handle business.

"Aight, listen up because I am not going to say what I got to say more than once," Joveezy said, looking at his goons in front of him. "Everyone needs to play they part. It's that simple. No fuck ups, no slip ups. Upon doing surveillance of the target we after, I took the liberty of getting a copy of the blueprints of the warehouse, pinpointing entrance and exits in case we need to get out fast. So, now we got the layouts of the inside of the building."

Joveezy took the papers out of the envelope and passed them to his righthand, Ced, who passed them on to everyone else. Each person had a cop of the blueprint sitting in front of them.

"This warehouse has four loading docks on the far back side where the trucks are going to be. There is going to be two U-Haul trucks unloading the merch. From the surveillance done, there is one driver and one guard for each truck plus an additional four guards – two for the front entrance, two at the side. Both trucks contain shipments. Inside the warehouse are three tiers. Upstairs on the third floor is where the office is and where our target is going to be. There are no cameras on the outside, but there are cameras on the inside. At least six to be exact."

Joveezy took a breath and looked around at everyone before he proceeded. "We don't know how many guards are inside, but there shouldn't be too many – at least twelve people, plus our target, and maybe two other people with him in his office. They won't be drawing attention because of the operation they have going on, but that doesn't mean that they won't be highly alert, so still be on point and watch each other's backs," Joveezy continued.

Ced got up from the table and went to the portrait hanging on the wall and slid it to the side. Behind the portrait was a steel door with a pin code. He entered a six-digit pin code, and the door buzzed open. Inside the room was a large, walk-in, storage area with shelves and kennel cages full of artillery and gadgets from suits to bulletproof vest. There were guns, rifles, grenades, ammunition, etc.

"Aight, let's gear up and get ready to take a ride," Joveezy told his crew. "Make sure you grab a walkie talkie and a headset to communicate through."

Everyone took all they needed for the trip they were about to embark on. Two duffle bags were filled with night vision googles, flashbangs, smoke grenades, handguns, rifles, extra clips for both, and M-15 assault rifles with silencers attached. Flashlights were detached from the rifles and only green beams remained attached along with holographic infrared scopes.

"Vic, you and Mondo will drive us to the location," Joveezy informed. "We are only taking two black Ford vans. Everyone will pile into both vans, one duffle bag in each van. Twenty minutes away from the warehouse, make sure goggles are on and weapons are hot. Once there, Andre will cut the power to the building. Then, the games are on. In the meantime, let's roll out," he said.

Everyone headed upstairs and out back to the waiting black vans.

Chapter 4

The drive to Detroit was a quiet ride. Joveezy's mind was focused on the task at hand. It was a little past midnight by the time they reached their destination. Twenty minutes away, they all put on the necessary equipment for the job.

"When we hit the block, cut the lights off and pull over up the street from the warehouse. Vic and Mondo, when we hop out, give us fifteen minutes to handle these niggas outside and then pull up. Andre, when we get to the warehouse, you and Breeze go around back and cut the power. At the time the power gets cut, it is a priority that we make it inside the building and move fast," he stressed.

They pulled up onto the block the warehouse was located on. The lights on both vans went off, as they pulled over. The streets were quiet, and the streetlights were dim, but they shone bright enough for people who dared to walk down the sidewalk at this time of night.

In the distance, sirens could be heard along with passing cars on the downtown streets of Detroit's eastside.

"Aight, goons," Ced said through his headset. "Stick to the shadows. When we get to the warehouse, split up, two to a group, and spread out."

"When we take care of business, Banks and Rowdy will grab the truck when we load everything up and take them to storage and meet back at the spot," Joveezy explained. "Let's slide and handle business."

There was an alley leading to a field with an abandoned building. They made their way toward it because it was dark enough to hide them and was in the back of the warehouse. The abandoned building provided cover, as they moved through it and came out on the other side into another wide alley. As they stepped out of the abandoned building, they heard voices off in the distance.

"Hold up," Joveezy whispered into his mic. The bright light on the building of the warehouse made it difficult for him to make out anything visible, so he lifted the goggles onto his forehead.

Ced came up next to him and did the same.

"We got four bodies to our left. Lil Loko and Nuke, go back into the building and take a clear position to take them out. Make sure every shot counts," Joveezy told them. "Banks and Rawdy, head to the right and head toward the front and clear out the front and make your entrance there. Andre and Breeze, when Loko and Nuke take them niggas out, head left and cut the power. When the power goes out, we make our move," he stated.

Loko and Nuke made their way to the perfect position and took out the first four men with no problem. As the bodies dropped, Joveezy and Ced signaled for their goons to move out. Joveezy and Ced followed with Andre and Breeze in tow.

There was a power box located outside of the back entrance where the bodies were laying. Andre opened the box and removed the fuses once he shut the power off.

"Let's go. Let's go," Joveezy said into his mic.

Joveezy and Ced lowered their night vision googles back onto their faces and entered the building with Andre and Breeze behind them. The area they entered was a large storage room. Through the night vision goggles, they could see men running around outside the double doors, and two men stumbled into the storage area with guns at the ready, looking around and trying to feel their way around in the darkness.

"What the fuck happened to the power?" asked one of the armed men.

"I don't know, but Armando and Nico not answering their walkies, nor is Thomas and Mikey," replied the second man.

As the two men walked closer toward them, Joveezy and Ced took both the men out with head shots, and Andre and Breeze made their way through the double doors.

Flashbangs and smoke grenades went off as gunfire burst into sound. It sounded like a massacre had broken out. Joveezy and Ced entered onto the main floor. Andre and Breeze were making their way toward the stairs leading to the second-tier catwalks. By the front entrance, Banks and Rawdy were laying down cover fire on the main floor, as Joveezy and Ced took cover behind some old, broken-down machinery.

Joveezy looked up and saw that the office was located on the third floor of the warehouse. He'd misjudged his calculation on the security that would be present. "Thank God we came prepared," he said to himself.

Ced headed for a staircase nearby, and Joveezy followed.

"Big Homie, they going to the U-Haul trucks inside on the main floor," said Rawdy. "Me and Banks gonna stay close by them and make sure they don't take off in them."

"Aight," said Joveezy. "Loko and Nuke, where y'all at?" he questioned.

"We just entered the building," responded Loko.

"Cover fire on the floor and hold position."

Joveezy and Ced made it up the stairs and proceeded to make their way to the third tier where the office was at.

As the gunfire started to cease, Joveezy and Ced reached the office. They heard voices coming from behind the door. The voices spoke in Italian, and gunshots pierced the door in wild spurts.

Joveezy took a flashbang and launched it through the office window beside the door and took cover. Two seconds later, the bang came along with the flash. The men inside the room yelled out in pain and frustration, as they were temporary blinded by the flashbang.

Ced kicked the door open, and Joveezy entered the room. Five Italians and two armed guards were in the room hunched over, rubbing their eyes. Joveezy shot both the armed men and two of the Italian men who had pistols in their hands.

Ced rushed the other men and held them at gunpoint, while Joveezy scanned the room. Through his night vision goggles, he could see that the office was very simple – a desk with five duffle bags sitting on top of it, two couches, and a cabinet with liquor and a small ice machine with beverages. The wall had a larger mirror in between the couches and a foreign statue sitting in front of the mirror. But there was no safe to be seen in the room.

“Where the fuck is the safe?” Joveezy asked the Italian standing behind the desk.

“Who the fuck are you? asked the Italian. “Do you know who you are fucking with?”

“Do you think I give a fuck? Now, I’m a ask you one more time. Where the fuck is the safe?”

“You got balls coming in here demanding shit,” said \the Italian on the couch.

Ced shot him in the face, and his brains splattered on the third Italian sitting next to him. “Shut your bitch ass up, pussy,” Ced said to the now dead Italian, who laid slumped over on the couch.

“Dammit, you hoodlum mutha…” the first Italian hissed.

Joveezy hit him with the butt of the rifle before he could finish his last word.

“Aww, fuck.”

“Start talking,” Joveezy demanded.

“Aight, man. The safe behind the mirror.”

Joveezy grabbed the Italian and walked him to the mirror. The Italian said, “Man, I can’t see shit.”

"Oh, well. You right in front of the mirror anyway. Put your hands forward and you right on the money."

The Italian reached forward and grabbed the mirror and moved it to the side. Behind the mirror was a combination and key lock safe.

"Where the key at?" asked Joveezy.

"It's in the desk, on the right hand side of the drawer."

"Let's get it."

Joveezy led the Italian back to the desk. He opened the desk drawer. Inside the drawer was a key, a gold plated forty-five, and a manilla envelope.

"Be smart," Joveezy warned.

The Italian felt around in the drawer. His hands brushed the pistol, and Joveezy pressed his rifle deeper into his rib cage. The Italian moved his hand to the key and grabbed it.

Joveezy pulled the Italian away from the desk and led him back to the safe.

"I have to put the combination in first before I can turn the key," explained the Italian.

"Hurry up!"

The Italian turned the dial on the combination and entered the code. The numbers on the dial glowed, so he could see the numbers. Once the combination was entered, he inserted the key. The safe came open.

Joveezy shot the Italian with one blow to the head, and as his body hit the floor, Ced shot the remaining Italian sitting on the couch.

Joveezy looked around inside the safe with admiration.

"Jackpot," Ced said, looking in.

They walked into the safe. Inside were shelves and racks full of guns. Boxes and crates laid on top of each other on the floor. Altogether, there were sixteen boxes and crates, eight apiece. The gun racks each held a different variety of weapons – from Ak-47s, SK5s, Glocks, Uzis, machetes, Smith and Wessons, grenades, Tech-nines, Kill techs, vests, etc. On the shelves were boxes of ammunition, kilos of heroin, cocaine, molly. and pounds of exotic weed. Altogether, there were twenty-eight kilos of heroin, eighty kilos of cocaine, forty kilos of molly, one hundred thirty-nine pounds of exotic weed, and vacuum sealed packs of money in bundles.

Joveezy opened up one of the boxes, and there were small boxes inside. The small boxes contained Rolexes, Cartier watches, and diamond chains. The crate Ced opened contained Egyptian statues. They closed the boxes up, and Joveezy called over the radio for everyone to make their way up to help load up the trucks, so they could leave.

"Andre? Cut the power back on," he requested.

The lights came back on, as everyone made their way up to the office.

"Load everything up in the U-Hauls," said Ced. "Make it quick, so we can get up out of here."

All the merchandise in the safe was loaded into the trucks. Nothing in the safe was left behind. There were VCR recordings from the video cameras, and Joveezy took the tapes and the VCR. He took the manilla envelope that was in the drawer as well, curious to see what was inside.

Banks and Rawdy closed up the U-Hauls, and both got into the two trucks and pulled out of the warehouse. One van followed the U-Hauls to the storage, while the other made its way to the spot back in Ypsilanti

Chapter 5

Lacey was taken to a surgeon to be treated for the gunshot wound she took, which turned out to be just a flesh wound. She was stitched up, and the doctor was paid for his services and to keep quiet. Later, they arrived at one of Lacey's ranch style homes out in Dearborn, Michigan.

Her fiancé, Nightmare, bought the house for them as an engagement gift. It was costly because of the land that came with it, but it was well worth the seven-figure price because of how well hidden it was in a secluded area deep in the woods. The ranch had a huge barn and was full of Nightmare's goons and security for the land. She had horses and cars to choose from for every day of the week. Cameras decorated the land like ornaments, and there was an outdoor shooting range. A pool house was built and connected to the house with a gym inside.

Lacey had gotten word that her cousin, Joveezy, was up-and-coming in the underworld. She needed to get ahold of him later and handle some business. Right now, she needed to build an empire of her own and claim vengeance on Dominic's punk ass, and with Nightmare at her disposal and willing to do whatever she requested, she had the Jamaican hitta and his ruthless savage killas on standby, ready to destroy anything and everyone she deemed a problem or threat.

When she entered the house, it looked like a gun store with artillery displayed all over the place. AK-47s, AR-15s, combat 12-gauges, Glocks, Mac11s, and AR pistols were scattered across a long, antique, wooden table, and Nightmare's goons lounged around the living and dining rooms in light tactical gear like it was a gentleman's bar.

Lacey looked in utter disbelief at the things that occupied her living space. These niggas were hell and had no class or manners at all and needed someone to snap them back to reality.

The men were smoking weed, drinking, pigging out on fast food, and watching movies in the living room.

"Where the fuck y'all think y'all at?" Lacey yelled angrily.

"We chilling, baby girl," one of the goons responded.

"Where is Nightmare?" she asked. "And y'all need to clean this shit up and get my house back the way it was. As a matter of fact, don't y'all niggas got shit to do besides sit on y'all asses all day? And get them damn guns off my fucking antique table. Y'all niggas done lost y'all damn minds."

"First off, Nightmare in the back room, and we apologize for the mess, shawty," replied the same goon. "And if you got some work for us, then let us know, so we can handle that shit. I mean, we isn't here toting guns and shit for nothing. I'm ready to stretch a nigga."

Lacey looked at Menace, a savage with a hunger for murder and chaos. Menace had a bald fade and a gold grill, stood six one, and weighted two hundred and eighty pounds, all muscle. He was Nightmare's cousin and top enforcer.

"Y'all niggas betta not get on my nerves. I'm already having a bad day," Lacey told them.

Menace laughed. "Aight, we got you. We just anxious to put in work right now. The sooner, the better, and then we can lay all the way back until the next job."

Lacey didn't like Menace, but he was good at what he did. He had a military background, so he was good with weapons and knew how to hunt. And his hand-to-hand combat was nasty.

She turned to leave the living room and went to find Nightmare in the bedroom.

Nightmare was in the bedroom with the lights dimmed. He stood by the picture window, peering out at the horses grazing in the night and the guards patrolling the ranch ground, some with rottweilers, some with a companion. His mind was on the events that took place tonight with Lacey amongst other things.

As he looked out into the night, he began to think about his past. Growing up on the eastside of Detroit had been rough. The slums had taken him under its core and showed him the ropes and how to survive and thrive. He was a shot-caller now, the head honcho, and was now able to afford anything he pleased. Niggas had no choice but to respect him, and now that he and Lacey were fucking with each other, it created even more of an issue with her ex, Dominic, who was a major problem. He didn't care though and wanted to show her as well as anyone else who doubted him that he could reign in the streets and do it better

Nightmare had taken Lacey into his life and had her by his side ever since. Because of her, he became more successful, and that alone made him a top target, almost costing him his life. It opened up his eyes, making him become a meaner nigga, and killing fueled the iniquity in him and opened Pandora's Box.

"Hey, baby," Lacey said, coming into the dimly lit bedroom.

Nightmare turned to face his woman. "Hi, baby, how are you feeling?" he asked softly. "Are you okay?"

Seeing him standing by the window with the look of hurt and concern on his face did something to her. He was shirtless with a muscular physique, and tattoos decorated his skin.

Lacey approached her lover and embraced him. "I'm okay, baby! I'm a little sore from the flesh wound, but it's nothing major."

"That nigga gone pay big time," he replied coldly.

"Yes, in due time," she responded, laying her head onto his chest.

Her mind stared to roam, as the demons inside of her started to stir. She was just as pissed at missing the opportunity to murder Dominic for setting her up like he did and lying to her about having Madame Charity. Now, she started to wonder if Dominic had something to do with her kidnapping. She thought he loved her. So, why would he betray her like he did? To make matters worse, Ariel, Dominic's bitch, was walking around in her shoes. It still bothered Lacey greatly that she had been replaced. She found out about Ariel after her return. Dominic had been her true love, or so she thought.

While she was held captive, she'd dreamed about him nonstop, but it seemed that he was still having the time of his life, while she was abducted. And now, he was trying to kill her, so any remnants of feelings she still had for him vanished when he tried to murder her.

Lacey tried to shake the events of what happened away. Nightmare had her heart now, but he would never be like Dominic, no matter how heartless, rich, and powerful he became. Nightmare had an army she needed, and he was there for her when she had no one. So, in return, she fucked him and sucked him passionately, and she gave everything she had into her relationship with him. But no matter how fast he was coming up and positioning himself in the underworld, she still had dominance and willpower over him and was ready to cut him off quickly if he played crazy.

Lacey had a devilish scheme that she was ready to implement. She wanted to hit Dominic where it would hurt him the worst. Getting at that bitch, Ariel, would be the pressure point at drawing out Dominic.

***

The black-on-black Porsche Cayman that Lacey drove was a birthday gift from Nightmare. He felt that she needed something fast but nice to drive in when cruising the streets of downtown Detroit. And it was Lacey's kind of car to cruise in and hit up all the well-known bars and nightclubs on the strip.

She drove to the Shadow bar, a popular scene to hit up and vibe with all kinds of people. The night was jumping with action, and she was loving the scenery. The Shadow bar was well-known to anybody who loved to have fun, and they were always live on the radio. The music blared some of the hottest local and non-local rappers and R&B artists like Dej Loaf, Peezy, Icewear Vezzo, Tee Grizzley, Baby Money, Moneybagg Yo, Glorila, 42 Dugg, Bryson Tiller, Chris Brown, and Mary J Blige.

Lacey pulled up to the spot in her sporty ride, and it immediately turned heads and got attention. There was a long line outside, and the bouncers wee big, black niggas who looked like they would bust heads wide open if the opportunity presented itself. Lacey stepped out of the car, placing her Red Bottoms onto the sidewalk and looking gorgeous in a tight fitting, black, Louis Vuitton mini dress.

Lacey was accompanied by her best friends and homegirls, Dee-Dee, Tonya, and Angelica. Dee-Dee and Tonya had mocha skin tones. Dee-Dee was five nine, wore micro braids, and had on a white Gucci dress. Tonya was five seven, had a full sleeve of tattoos, and wore a one sleeved mini dress by Ferragamo, and Angelica was a redbone chick. She was six one with light freckles on her face and wore Gucci glasses and a brown, tight fitting Gucci dress. Her hair was in a bun.

Lacey gave the main bouncer five hundred dollars to let her and her girls through. When she stepped into the bar, it was lively and packed with well-dressed people. But Lacey didn't come to party and mingle. She was there for a reason and was content on implementing her scheme. She scanned the crowed, searching for Ariel. From the information she'd retrieved, she knew this to be one of her favorite scenes to pop out at.

Lacey and her friends went to the bar to order some drinks. She kept her senses on alert, wary about her surroundings due to the last incident with Dominic.

After an hour and a half of partying among the partygoers, Lacey's plan on running into Ariel and reeling her into the folds was a dead end. Since Ariel was a no show, Lacey left the Shadow bar with her homegirls following right behind her.

Chapter 6

The next night, Lacey hit up some more clubs and bars downtown and then the casinos. She made an effort to hit up every spot, hoping to catch Ariel.

Lacey decided to check out one more spot, and she finally got her prize at Déjà vu strip club. Déjà vu was on smack mode tonight. All the major players and dope boys were there and preoccupied with the ladies. It was late, midnight, and Lacey spotted Ariel sitting in the VIP section with her entourage. She was dressed in a red, Prada, knee-high dress and had long, brown hair and cocoa brown skin to match her curvy body. She was drop dead gorgeous and got more attention than the strippers. Yeah, she was a head turner. It was no wonder Dominic played her like he did with no hesitation. Ariel had two of her girls with her, and they had two bottles of sparkling Ace of Spades in ice buckets.

Lacey watched Ariel closely with Dee-Dee, Tonya, and Angelica standing close by, ready to get at Ariel. From the attention she was receiving, it was clear that she was a regular at the strip club. The DJ even gave her a shout out.

"This bitch really think she doing something," Lacey said to no one in particular. "Who the fuck she think she is?"

"What's up? Let's whoop this bitch right now," Dee-Dee suggested eagerly.

"Naw, not right now. There's too many eyes. Now that we know she here, we gone watch her like a hawk. And when it's time, we gone make our move. Until then, just relax a little."

Lacey continued to watch the scene play out. Soon, Ariel's VIP section started to gather with a small crowd of people as a private party took place. The girls downed the bottles, laughed, danced, and took pleasure in the attention they were getting from the men and some of the strippers. The women looked extra vagrant in their club attire, each showing off flesh and more booty that would drive even females crazy with lust.

Lacey looked at the females in disgust, especially the one who took her man, her place, and thought she was a boss bitch running shit. Ariel wasn't running shit; she was nothing but a gold-digger and sack chaser living off of Dominic and his wealth. Lacey was ready to shoot the bitch in the face, point blank on the spot, with each passing second. Just the sight of her made her heart harden even more.

Lacey had seen enough though, and she made her way to Ariel's VIP area to make her presence known. Her homegirls were in tow, right behind her like a shadow. She reached the VIP section where Ariel and her entourage partied, dancing in their Red Bottoms and flirting with some of the men. One of the females had a guy in between her legs, giving her head. Ariel had her own personal security, but Lacey didn't care, as she approached the lit group.

As she came near, the guard in a black suit stepped in front of Lacey and her homegirls, extending his hands to stop them in their tracks.

"Sorry, ladies, this is a private VIP area," he said.

"Bitch ass nigga, I don't give a fuck about none of that. I need to holla at that bitch right there." Lacey nodded in Ariel's direction.

"Well, if you weren't invited, you not getting through here. It's that simple," he replied with anger and agitation.

"Who the fuck you think you talking to?"

"Look, shawty, bounce up out of here and move around. I'm trying to be kool about this shit."

"Nigga, what's that supposed to mean?! Do you not know who the fuck you dealing with?"

"To be frank wit' you, I don't give a fuck, now move the fuck around because you ain't coming through here."

"Boy, you need to watch yo' fucking mouth when you speaking to her." Dee-Dee approached the guard. Tonya and Angelica stepped forward too, ready to pounce on the guard.

Ariel's attention was drawn to all the commotion that was going on at the entrance of her VIP section. She noticed a beautifully dressed woman that caught her eye.

"What is going on?" asked one of Ariel's friends.

"Some jealous bitch trying to cause a scene and ruin my private party," Ariel said. "Let me go see what's up with this bitch right quick." She walked over to where the argument was happening.

Lacey grinned and locked eyes with Ariel as she approached.

"Excuse me, bitch, is there a problem?" Ariel asked sharply.

"Bitch, you betta watch yo' mouth, ho," said Tonya, cocking her fist back, ready to strike, as Lacey grabbed her wrist.

"Hold on, girl. Let me handle this," Lacey stated. She repeated Tonya's statement. "Do you know who I am?"

"No, I don't. Should I?"

"Bitch, let me introduce myself. I am Dominic's ex that the nigga left for dead, and you can tell that nigga I'm coming for him and you too, bitch!" Lacey said. "And best believe shit about to change around this bitch. See, right now, you lucky because if I wanted to, I could get to you with no problem, and your bitch ass security won't do shit. Let the name Lacey set in your brain for a while."

At the mention of the name Lacey, Ariel's eyes became large, and fear settled in. She had heard about Lacey through the grapevine, and the streets knew she wasn't the bitch to be fucked with. Her reputation was hardcore, and even killas knew to tread lightly around her. She had been through it all. She'd been to war with the best of them and came out on top, been shot on multiple occasions, kidnapped, and betrayed. She had endured all that, even lost her baby brother to a violent death, and was still standing tall and healed faster than most.

Lacey spoke calmly. "Yeah, bitch, take a good look at the true queen."

Ariel could hardly look into Lacey's light brown eyes. Her presence sent chills down her spine. Ariel could feel her heart start to beat uncontrollably from the stone-cold fear that set in. And with Lacey's entourage standing right beside her, looking as deadly as she was, Ariel knew that her festive night would turn into a deadly one.

"Look, I don't want any problems with you," Ariel said with trembling fear in her voice.

"Bitch, your problem started when you started fucking with Dominic."

Ariel's girlfriends stood up behind their friend as if they had her back and were ready to step. Lacey looked at them and could tell that they weren't ready to go against her and her squad. They were just around because Ariel treated them to a good time. These bitches were nobodies.

"Bitches, what y'all tryna do? Y'all ready to meet your maker?" Angelica asked the females standing behind Ariel.

"We don't want no problem please," Ariel repeated. She looked over her shoulder toward her friends. "Y'all, chill. This is not that. They the wrong ones to play with."

"I'm glad we got that understood," Lacey retorted.

Ariel was ready to get on the phone and call Dominic. The lump that formed in her throat was heavy. She was ready to piss herself from fear. She was put in a situation that she was not ready for by a long shot. Ariel was just a normal girl who got by how she could, although her mother and father had lots of money. Yeah, she had seen her share of fights, but Lacey was a whole different ball game and out of her league.

Dominic and the people he was associated with had their hands in murder, kidnappings, extortion, racketeering, dealing in drugs, and the list went on and on. But Dominic was part of who Ariel was now.

Security started to show up due to the commotion taking place. Lacey had busted up Ariel's party. The look in Ariel's eyes told Lacey that she had gotten her message across, but it wasn't enough. She blew Ariel a kiss and walked away with her girls right behind her, leaving Ariel petrified.

The minute Lacey was outside the strip club, she told her homegirls that they would lie in wait for Ariel to come out and then get at her a few miles from the club.

Back in the strip club, Ariel and her friends were desperate to end the night. Ariel was screaming into her phone, as she exited the strip club, looking around in panic. "Dominic, this bitch had the audacity to show up and threaten me. Supposedly, your ex is pissed at me for fucking with you… No, she gone now… Yeah, I'm sure. Okay, I'm on my way now."

As Ariel and her girls pulled out of the parking lot, unbeknownst to them, a car followed not too far behind.

Twenty minutes into the drive, the car following bumped lightly into Ariel's car, and she was forced to pull over on the side of the road. The street was quiet, and there was no traffic.

Ariel and her girls got out the car drunkenly. When they approached the back of the car, the high beams came on on the car that bumped them, and the back car door flew open. As Ariel and her friends shielded their eyes from the high beams, footsteps approached hurriedly.

"Gotcha, bitch," said a familiar female voice.

"Oh, my God," screamed Ariel as gun shots rang out. She flinched as bullets whizzed past her ear.

Bodies could be heard hitting the ground as she screamed. The next shot that came silenced her completely, and darkness clouded her vision.

Chapter 7

Joveezy woke up around noon in the home he'd bought in West Willow in Ypsilanti, Michigan. The big red star was high in the sky, and the block was teeming with activity in the summer heat.

He sat up on the edge of his bed, head pounding from the last two days of celebration they had for a successful lick. He got up and was heading to the bathroom when he accidently bumped into the nightstand. A manila envelope fell to the floor. He picked it up and looked at it, trying to remind himself what was inside before setting the envelope back down on the nightstand.

Inside the bathroom, he ran the shower until the temperature was just right and got in. For the first fifteen minutes, he let the water run down his body, reminiscing about the play that went down and the merchandise they had back in storage.

When he and Ced went to get a good look at the layout of stuff they'd hit the Italians for, they inventoried everything they had. The U-Haul trucks were taken out of state and burned inside out.

Joveezy and Ced stayed up all day and well into the next morning separating and calculating. The had enough guns to start a small army, and they were stacked with drugs. All the products would have to be sold out of town and farther down South. The five duffle bags they got had fifty thousand dollars in each bag, all in cerements of twenty. The vacuum sealed packs of money they found came out to be six hundred and fifty thousand dollars in twenties, fifties, and hundreds, which were divided amongst the participants in the lick.

Joveezy remembered Ced examining the statues, while he was inventorying the jewelry they had, when he heard a loud crash. He looked over at Ced and saw the statue broken on the ground in pieces and spilling out of the statue was more drugs. They looked at each other and started breaking the remaining statues. In total, there were fourteen crates, not including the eight in the office safe, that were taken from the warehouse. Each crate contained four Egyptian statues, and inside each statue were two kilos of meth.

He snapped back to reality, finished up his shower, and got out to brush his teeth. When he heard his cell phone ring in the bedroom, he rushed to go answer it.

"Hello," he answered.

"Hey, Daddy! What's up? Where you been? I thought you were going to be back when you handled business."

"I am, baby. I just got sidetracked. I promise I'ma slide through today, and you got me for the next week."

"Aight, bae. I miss you and want you so bad right now."

"I promise you got me, Lisa. That's my word," he said, going into his top drawer to grab a pair of Calvin Klein boxers and socks.

When he closed the drawer, the manilla envelope fell to the floor again. He picked it up and set it back on the nightstand next to his Glock17 and picked up the Glock.

Joveezy took the Glock to a tall, built-in, wall safe and scanned his fingerprint before entering a six-digit pin code. Inside the safe, he switched out the Glock 17 for a Glock 34. From the safe, he also took out a gold Rolex watch, a gold choker, and three gold Cuban linked chains with crushed canary yellow diamonds with specks of red crushed diamonds scattered about. He closed the safe and headed for the closet.

"Daddy, I want to go out to eat tonight, if that's okay with you?" Lisa asked.

"Yeah, we can," he responded, picking out an outfit for the day." Where do you want to go?"

"I want to go somewhere nice but not too classy. How about we do seafood or steak?" she asked excitedly.

"That sounds like a plan."

"Okay, I will see you when you get here. I love you, Daddy. Bye."

"I love you too," he replied before ending the call.

Joveezy put on a pair of Christian Dior jeans and red Dior T-shirt with the word Dior in white lettering across the chest. He threw on his jewelry and grabbed a holster for his Glock and threw the Glock into the holster before he put it on his hip.

He grabbed a Louis Vuitton backpack and stuffed it with eighty thousand in cash from a medium safe in the back of his closet. On the way out, he grabbed his phone and the manilla envelope off the nightstand.

Joveezy went into the garage and at the door greeted his two French bull mastiffs, Tango and Bonnie. He had them both fixed so that they didn't breed. Their only purpose were to act on command and protect his home as well as his life. He let Tango into the house, closed the door, and locked it before setting the house alarm.

Off the garage wall, he grabbed a short chain linked leash and latched Bonnie onto it. He walked her to the red Trackhawk parked in the garage next to the Hellcat and let her onto the back floor. He sat the Louis Vuitton backpack next to her, closed the back door, and got in front. Before he opened the garage to leave, Joveezy opened the manilla envelope and looked at the contents inside.

The contents contained photos of the Italians they hit and a Jamaican guy. In another photo, a female was outside of a casino, talking to the same Italians in the previous photo, and next to her was that Jamaican dude again. The female looked familiar to him. And then it hit him. The face he was staring at in the photo was his cousin, Lacey. There were more photos left, but he didn't want to look at the rest. As he put the photo back inside the envelope, a piece of paper stuck out from between two photos.

Joveezy grabbed the paper and read what was on it. The piece of paper had an address. No name, no city, or zip code. Just a house number, street name, and a message that said, "Under the moonlight, you will find my heart and soul."

He sat in the car for a few minutes, trying to comprehend what the message meant. His mind was racing, and he was curious about what was at that address. In the meantime, he would put it aside and later dig a little deeper into the situation and find out what the message revealed.

All in all, he had a gut feeling that he had a serious problem on his hands, and he would need to get with Ced and discuss the issue. Whoever was watching Lacey and the Italians was sure to be on to him. And he needed to figure out who they were.

He pulled out of the garage and drove away, heading to meet up with Lisa. The drive from West Willow to Crystal Creek seemed long. So much was running through Joveezy's mind that he didn't notice the white Rubicon tailing two cars behind him.

Joveezy pulled into a BP gas station on Washtenaw Avenue to fill up the Trackhawk. While he was standing at the pump, he noticed the white Rubicon with black tint and black rims pulling in. The Jeep pulled two pumps over and just sat there.

After Joveezy pumped the gas, he went into the gas station to the cold freezer and grabbed two Red Bulls and a Monster energy drink. Then, he went to the snack aisle and grabbed a box of Slim Jims. As he walked away from the snack aisle, he took a glance at the Rubicon to see if he could see who was behind the windshield. He could see two people in front and a glimpse of the person in the backseat behind the driver. The driver was a white male, the passenger was Black, and the backseat passenger was a white male as well.

He went to the counter to pay for his items and grabbed a box of White Owls in the silver pack. When he exited the store, Joveezy looked over at the Jeep and headed to his Trackhawk. He got in and backed away from the gas pump so that he could drive past the Jeep to get a look at the license plate. The Jeep had no plates.

Joveezy pulled out of the gas station and drove back toward the southside and got on his cell phone. When he looked in the rearview, the Jeep was following him.

"Hello," said the caller on the other end.

"Aye, Blood, we got a problem. There's a white Rubicon tailing me with no plates. I think they been on me since I left the house in the Willows."

"Damn, my nigga, you ain't peeped them when you left out? They probably stick-up boys." \

"Naw, my nigga, I didn't, and I don't think they stick-up boys. They too content," Joveezy informed with concern in his voice.

"Who you think them niggas is then? And what you need me to do?"

"I don't know, Blood, but I'm bout to head your way. They gone be right behind me, so when I slide through, cut them off, so I can shake 'em."

"Aight, stay on the phone while you do a drive through, and I'ma let you know when to hit the pedal to the floor."

"Aight, bet. I'm bout forty-five seconds away."

As Joveezy navigated his way to Mike, he couldn't shake the feeling of being followed by people he didn't know. He glanced in the rearview mirror and noticed that the white Jeep was speeding up.

"Shitt!" he said to himself, as he put his foot on the gas to accelerate.

As the Trackhawk sped up, ahead of him, a dark sedan coming from the opposite direction cut him off, blocking him from getting around them, forcing him to slam on brakes.

In that same moment, a tan sedan and a black Dodge Durango pulled up next to the Jeep Rubicon, red and blue lights flashing, blocking his ability to reverse, and suddenly, he found himself surrounded by law enforcement agents.

"Damn, bro, it's the Feds!" he said to Mike before ending the call

He immediately hit a button on his radio, and the device slid out like a tray. Joveezy threw the manilla envelope and his gun with the holster onto the deep-dish tray and hit the button again to close it. He held the button for four seconds until a light flashed on the button and went away, indicating that the tray was locked.

Bonnie raised her head, growling.

"Easy, girl, easy," he said to the mastiff.

Joveezy looked out in front of him and in the rearview mirror. A dozen men in black tactical gear, DEA, and all with FBI imprinted on the front breast pockets, badges showing around their necks and guns out, charged his truck, screaming, "Get out the vehicle. Get out the vehicle now! Exit with your hands up in the air! Do it now!" yelled the FBI agent behind him on the bullhorn.

"Dog! Dog!" yelled one of the agents, shutting the door.

"Don't shoot my dog, man, please," begged Joveezy. He felt a knee pressing into his back and his arms being folded behind him.

"Control that dog before we shoot that muthafucker," ordered the agent pinning him down.

"Aight, man, let me up," he requested.

The agent put zip ties on his wrist before letting him up. He walked him to the other side of the truck and slightly opened the door a crack.

"Hush, girl, heel," Joveezy said to Bonnie.

Immediately, Bonnie calmed down and laid back down next to the Louis backpack.

"What's in that backpack that dog guarding?" questioned the FBI agent with the bullhorn, grabbing the Louis bag with caution. The agent opened the backpack, and stacks of money fell out.

"What are you doing with all this money?" asked the agent.

"That's my business, not yours," Joveezy said.

"Cut the games, you smart ass bitch. We know who you are."

"Y'all don't 'know shit, maggot ass pussies."

"We know you're a killa and a notorious drug dealer. We been doing surveillance on you for the past month now," explained the agent.

"Yeah, yeah, that's it? A month? And y'all got all y'all need in that little time? Man, cut it out," said Joveezy. "I'm a successful businessman. I own a barbershop and house and have investments in franchises. And that money came from a loan at the bank. You can call my bank and ask."

"Yeah, we might just do that and look into your other claims as well," said the agent.

"Well, until then, I ain't got shit to say." Joveezy kept his mouth closed. He didn't utter another word during his arrest.

One of the agents held a dog catcher pole and grabbed Bonnie with it to remove her from the vehicle. She was growling and snapping at the pole catcher, as they put her in a medium size dog cage and put her into the back of an FBI truck. FBI agents proceeded to tear his truck apart, searching for incriminating evidence, but there was nothing for them to find. They even checked up under the hood of his truck. Frustrated, they shoved him into the backseat of the Durango.

"Take him back to headquarters for questioning."

Joveezy smirked because he knew they had nothing on him.

Chapter 8

Lacey's moans echoed throughout the bedroom. As her orgasms overpowered her ability to stay in control, her hands gripped the bed sheets tightly. She felt Nightmare's long tongue dipping passionately into her dripping wet pussy, as his lips sucked on her clit as if it were a sweet mango. Naked and vulnerable in his grasp, she wrapped her legs around him, fucking his face and rotating her hips. Nightmare's well-defined arms raised her legs into the air and spread them wider, exposing her dripping wetness even more, and he went to work on her pussy like it was a full course meal, his tongue lapping up her juices.

Lacey closed her eyes and enjoyed her pussy being sucked profusely. The more he ate her out, the wetter she became. His tongue game was unbearable and had her mind blown. The only sounds in the room were her moans and the slurping of her juices being tasted and swallowed.

The oral sex then stopped, and Lacey found her legs being spread wider, giving her lover full access to her passionate garden any way he wanted. He leaned forward against Lacey, positioning himself between her thick, shapely thighs.

Nightmare's thrust was powerful. His body pressed down on top of hers, allowing her to feel like she was being swallowed up by his muscular frame.

Lacey's nails dug slightly into Nightmare's back, as he thrust deeper into her, scaling deeply down his back, drawing some blood from the scratches she made. "Fuck me!" she found herself crying out. "Oh, God, please fuck me!"

The sex was focused, and the dick digging inside of her made her want to go crazy

Lacey raised her legs farther in the air, grabbing the back of her knees to hold her position and allow Nightmare to go even deeper.

He grabbed her legs and brought her knees to her shoulders, almost touching the back of her head, and began to give her long and deep strokes.

Lacey's breath caught in her chest. "Oh, fuck! Shit! Yes!" she moaned out, as she was being fucked out of her mind.

Nightmare pulled out of her and flipped her onto her stomach. He raised her ass in the air just enough to position himself and slammed into her.

Lacey screamed out at the force, as Nightmare crammed in and out of her.

"Oh, shit, bae, please slow down. That shit hurts when you dig in me like that," she moaned.

She brought one knee up under her to get into a better position in hopes of easing the pain that she was enduring, but it only made him go harder.

Lacey didn't know what to do. She wanted to run and tap out, but the pleasurable pain felt good too. She was so wet that a small puddle began to form on the bed sheets. The dick that Nightmare gave her had Lacey beat, as she came and squirted all over him.

Nightmare started to grunt, as he felt the pressure build. His dick jerked uncontrollably inside of her, as his cum exploded deep inside her. He laid on top of her, as they both tried to catch their breath.

He rolled off of her, and Lacey laid her head on his chest.

"So, what mischief have you been getting yourself into?" asked Nightmare.

"Just some errands I had to run, small shit, and hit up a few clubs," she answered. "Why? What's up?"

"Just wondering. One of my boys said they seen you at the strip club ready to beat a bitch down. What was that shit about?"

"Nothing, bae. She was a bitch from the past who brought back memories, and it had to be hashed out, but she got big headed," Lacey explained with a grin.

"I'm just tryna make sure you not being messy with these bitches, but I know you got this," he stated.

"Yeah, I got this, love. Why wouldn't I?"

"Baby, lately, you been on a hell spree, and before you know it, a big war is going to spark more out of control than it already is."

"Well, then maybe I want war, nigga, so these fuck niggas will understand the power and meaning behind it," Lacey retorted angrily, getting out of bed.

"Hold on, baby. It ain't even like that seriously. I'm with you all the way," he assured.

"If you with me, why I feel like you are questioning or doubting me?" inquired Lacey, eyeing him suspiciously.

"I'm not. But look, let's just drop it because I'm not trying to upset you."

"Yeah, it's better that way," Lacey agreed, removing a pack of Newport's from her handbag.

She lit a cigarette and took a deep pull from it. After she'd smoked the cigarette halfway, she put it out and went to take a shower.

The shower was hot, as she stood under the water. Lacey's mind was darkened with hate and unforgiveness, and the thirst to see blood shed lived deep within her raging heart.

Lacey's mind drifted back to the day she was kidnapped.

It was her nineteenth birthday. Dominic had rented out a hall on the westside of Detroit and threw her a big party. The hall was where big events and wedding parties took place. Everyone that was invited to the party was close friends, family, and major players, even local rappers.

The party was jumping, and Dominic made sure that Lacey got everything she asked for and more. She danced with her homegirls and drank the most expensive bottles of champagne and liquor. And the weed was plentiful.

An hour before the party ended, Lacey received gifts and opened them. She got diamond earrings, necklaces, money, and dresses that cost ten thousand or more. But the priciest gift was from Dominic. He bought her a black Ferrari Spyder with pink interior and as a bonus gift, a white Rolls Royce Ghost with pink interior and gold stitching.

Lacey was speechless at the sight of her new rides. The gifts she received were already too much. She jumped in Dominic's arms, crying from joy.

After the party, Dominic told Lacey to pick out what vehicle she was going to drive that night, and the other car would be taken back to the house along with her birthday gifts.

Lacey chose to take to the Ferrari, and she asked her best friend, Carmela, to accompany her for the rest of the night.

Her and Carmela drove off into the night to hit up some casinos, and as they neared the main street, Lacey didn't notice the Mercedes van following her.

She'd decided to take the scenic route through a few neighborhood streets to avoid a long journey to her destination when the Mercedes van sped around her and cut her off, causing her to swerve and crash her Ferrari into a parked car. Lacey was momentarily dazed, as men from the van jumped out and ran toward her and Carmela. By the time she realized what was happening, she was snatched out of the car along with Carmela and dragged to the van. She heard Carmela screaming out her name, as she was taken too.

Lacey looked around at the men who were wearing masks, and that was when she knew something bad was about to happen. She started to fight the men off, but they were too strong. As she continued to struggle and shout, one of the men punched her, and she was stunned for a few seconds.

As she watched in horror, one of the men that had Carmela pulled out a gun and shot her dead center in the forehead. Lacey screamed as she was thrown into the back of the van. As the van doors started to close and the men piled up in the van, surrounding her, she was hit hard in the temple, and everything went black.

When Lacey came to, she was tied up and gagged with a pillowcase over her head. Fear and panic started to creep in upon her awakening. She heard footsteps moving toward her, and the object covering her head was pulled off. The room she sat in was dimly lit. There were three men in the room with her that she could see. As she looked around, the room smelled of musk and sex. It was hot, and the walls were dirty, as the paint started to peel away. There was a bed on the other side of the room and a camera in the corner, facing the bed. Across from the bed was a door with a window boarded up next to it.

Behind her, she heard water running. The water cut off, and a door opened. An older, white man with salt and pepper colored hair came into view. He was at least five feet eight inches tall, fat, and had a bulky build. He wore a grey Lacoste suit, Lacoste loafers, with a gold Rolex. The cologne he wore was a spice and Gucci mixed fragrance.

In his hands, he carried a small satchel. He set the satchel on the bed and opened it. Inside the satchel were small vials, scalpels, syringes, pills, and packets of a crystal-like substances and powder. There were also small instruments such as spoons, bandages, and gauze.

Lacey's mind was racing, wondering who this man was and what they wanted with her and what they were going to do with her. With all the stuff the man had in the small suitcase, he looked like he was a doctor.

The man laid out a syringe, a spoon, and a small packet that looked like brown tar. He emptied the contents onto the spoon and added water. The man then pulled a lighter from his pocket and heated up the bottom of the spoon until the watery substance started to bubble. After that, he put a piece of cotton ball on the spoon to soak up the substance and used the spoon to cook up the contents from the cotton ball. He set the syringe down and pulled out his cell phone and pressed a number he had on speed dial.

"Yeah, everything's ready to go," the man said to the person on the other end. "Yes, she's awake now."

He hung up the phone and nodded to the men standing next to Lacey. They walked toward her and untied her from the chair. As soon as one of her arms came loose, she struck one of the men in the face, breaking his nose, before they grabbed her.

She struggled against the men, as they carried her to the bed and held her down. The older, white man grabbed the syringe and thumped his fingertips against the side of it to make sure there weren't any bubbles. As he moved toward her, the door opened.

"Wait," said the stranger who entered the room.

The voice that spoke was a female's voice, and as she came into view, Lacey could see her appearance. The woman was beautiful – tall, about six one in height, high yellow skin, jet-black, straight hair – but her eyes were as dark as the night. Something about her sent chills up and down Lacey's spine. She had a foreign accent, like Middle Eastern or Colombian.

"I've been looking forward to meeting you for some time now," said the woman. "Me and you have a mutual acquaintance, but for now, it's just about me and you. Remove the gag."

One of the men holding Lacey down removed the gag from her mouth.

"Heeellpp," Lacey screamed.

"Hellppp," the lady screamed, mocking Lacey. "No one can hear you or help you, sweetheart. So, cut that shit out."

"What do you want from me?" asked Lacey, crying.

"What I want, I have now, and that's you. You will bring me a lot of money."

"If it's money you want, I have plenty of it. Just please let me go."

"No, no, no. Your money means nothing when I have my own. Your body and the will to use it is what I want, and you will use it for pleasure. You will bring me more money with it."

'No, please don't do this," Lacey begged. "My man will come looking for me. You don't know what you are getting yourself into."

"Oh, please. I hear that shit so much that I'm so sick of it. Besides, your man won't come."

"Yes, he will, and you will pay for what you did to my cousin, bitch."

"Yeah, yeah, yeah, all in due time, sweet face. Right now, Madame Charity owns you, and I will get what I want," she said, chickling, before nodding to the older, white man.

The white man moved forward with the syringe.

Lacey started kicking and screaming. "No, please don't do this. Please," she begged again.

The men holding her down put their weight on her more to keep her from moving so much, as the older, white man found a vein and stuck the needle into Lacey's arm.

"My God, she has lovely veins," he said.

"No," Lacey mumbled, still struggling against her captives faintly. As the drug started to take effect, she started to calm down immediately. The rush from the substances the man injected her with started to numb her feelings. Lacey's mind was in the clouds as she felt a high that she had never felt before. The feeling she felt was like nothing she'd ever experienced. The fear and panic, along with the emotions that overwhelmed her, went away, and she was filled with a tingling and sexual rush. She tried to fight what was controlling her mind, but it was no use.

"Have fun with her, fellas, but please don't damage my property too badly, or it's gonna cost you. She still has money to make me," Madame Charity said before exiting the room.

The men stripped away Lacey's clothing and had their way with her for hours. By the next day, she was moved to another room and fed more drugs to keep her submissive, while different men came in and out of the room she was in and fucked her. Some defiled her in ways she never thought possible, but she was so high that she didn't process all that was happening.

Lacey came back to reality, as she heard her name being called. The memory of what happened to her held her in a trance, gripping her mind like glue. She shook it off.

"Lacey!?" yelled Nightmare with a hint of frustration and panic in his voice, as he entered the bathroom.

Lacey peeked her head out of the shower. "What, bae?" she asked.

"We got a big fucking problem. Somebody hit our shipment."

"Which one and when?"

"The one we had set up with the Italians. The got hit a couple days ago, and they got hit hard. Marco and his brothers are dead too."

"Was it a police raid?" she asked.

"No, it was a robbery. Somebody knew about our shipment coming in," Nightmare informed.

"Well, do we know who it was?" Lacey questioned.

"No, the muthafuckas took the video feed from the cameras and both trucks full of merchandise. They cleared the safe too. Them niggas ain't leave shit behind but dead bodies," he said. "I got people looking into the situation now and asking around. We don't know if it was an inside job or not yet."

"Aight, well, we need to figure this shit out fast because we invested two million into this shipment that's worth well over five. I can't afford to lose, and Marco was one of our best connects. Hit up the Arabs and Caldrons and tell them to keep an eye and ear out for anybody who mysteriously made a big come up. Somebody gotta pay," she demanded.

"Aight," Nightmare said before leaving the bathroom.

Lacey cut off the shower and got out, pissed. As she was drying off, her cell phone rang. She picked it up and answered without looking at the caller ID.

"What?" she screamed with anger in her voice.

"Bitch, I'ma do more than kill you when I catch you. I'ma cut your stanking ass up and feed you to the meat grinder when I get my hands on you."

"Fuck you, Dominic. You was a dead man when you tried to kill me, you punk bitch, and let me find out you hit my connect," she screamed into the phone.

"I know you killed my bitch, and not only do you got me to deal with, you got other problems on your hands too, and I don't need your whack ass connects. I am the connect."

"Nigga, you ain't shit. Never was, never will be. And besides, I stay with more problems than I can count, so what's new?"

"You wanted Madame Charity that bad. Now you have her." He laughed. "Ariel was her daughter."

"Well, that's one bitch out the... Wait, so you was fucking this bitch's daughter, while that bitch held me captive and was having me raped and abused for money, you grimy ass nigga?"

"Bitch, how you think you got to that point? I fucked with you, so I could get to her. You were never my bitch. Hell, you were never my type. I just needed to earn your trust and heart, and once I had it, I had guaranteed ties with a wealthy and powerful crime family who could make me richer. All I had to do was marry her daughter, Ariel. My father and her mother were very close and had a contract together, and your jealous ass couldn't stay the fuck away," Dominic ranted. "You ruined everything."

“Fuck you, you punk ass faggot. I’m glad I was smart enough to take your money and put it elsewhere, dumbass. You made your bed with white rose petals, now die in it,” she said before ending the call.

Lacey walked out of the bathroom and got dressed. Nightmare was sitting on the bed, barking orders into the phone.

She walked over to him. “I need to handle some shit,” she said and kissed him on the lips before leaving.

Chapter 9

Two federal agents in charge of the investigation interrogated Joveezy for hours in a small, cramped, windowless room, trying to get him to talk and give them information. But Joveezy wouldn't talk. He knew they didn't have anything on him because if they did, they wouldn't be asking questions now and trying to put things together. Joveezy could see these federal agents needed him to talk. He wasn't about to become anyone's pawn. The federal agents made threats of a long prison sentence in the Feds if he didn't cooperate, but Joveezy laughed and continued to keep silent.

After the ongoing interrogation, Joveezy decided to talk, and what he said sent the federal agents in a frenzy.

"Look, it's obvious you don't have shit on me. You already said that the money you found in my truck was indeed a loan from my bank. So, what else are y'all expecting to get out of me? I don't know shit you all are talking about and could care less. As a matter of fact, I'm wasting my breath, so I want my lawyer present please and thank you." He looked at them with a smirk.

The lead federal agent assigned to the case came closer to him and leaned down close enough that his breath fell on the side of Joveezy's face, smelling like shit and onions.

"So, now you want your lawyer present, huh? Aight," he said, snatching Joveezy up by the collar. "Muthafucker, you're gonna talk, or I'ma make you talk."

The second federal agent in the room with them rushed forward and grabbed his partner. “Vincent, chill, man. What the fuck are you doing? Don’t let this thug get to you,” he told his partner.

Agent Vincent let Joveezy go before turning to his partner. “This thug knows something, Dom, and I’m going to find out what he knows. He thinks he’s outsmarting us, but I’m always a step ahead,” he said, turning back to Joveezy.

“Man, fuck all that. Is you gonna let me have my lawyer present or what?” he asked.

“Yeah,” Agent Vincent said before heading out the door with this partner following suit.

The door shut behind them, and Joveezy took a deep breath. His mind was running a marathon. He knew that they didn’t have enough to charge him with anything. So, the only thing they could do was hold him for forty-eight to seventy-two hours or let him go.

He figured they would hit his home in West Willow, while he was there being interrogated, but that house had nothing to offer, and all of his firearms were legally registered. There was nothing illegal in his home, and besides the eighty thousand, the only money left in his safe was less than ten thousand dollars.

It pays to be a successful businessman and have something to fall back on to cover your tracks, he thought.

Joveezy’s thinking was interrupted by the sound of the door opening up, and a federal agent stepped into the room.

“You’re free to go,” the agent told him.

Joveezy got up and was escorted out front of the building where his truck was parked. Another agent stood next to his truck with his French mastiff on a leash, and her face was covered with a muzzle to keep her from biting the agents.

Federal Agent Vincent came out of the building, carrying the Louis backpack with the money, and handed the bag to

Joveezy. "We will be watching you and watching you closely," he told him.

Joveezy looked him in the eyes. "I will be in contact with some of my lawyers and the mayor to let them know of your harassment," he said, smiling.

He then turned his back on the agent and grabbed the leash from the agent holding it. The federal agents walked back inside the building.

Joveezy opened up the truck to put Bonnie and his backpack in the back and noticed that his truck was a mess. The backseats were pulled off their tracks, and the radio was pulled out, but it wasn't open.

He got into the truck and put the radio back in its place and started up his truck before pulling away. As he drove a few blocks away, he hit the button on his radio, and the tray drawer slid out. All of its contents were still inside. He took his gun and placed it on his hip and placed the manilla envelope on the passenger seat. He took his phone out and noticed all of the missed calls he had from Mike, Lisa, and Ced.

He called Lisa and told her that he got caught up in a serious situation and that he would explain when he got there. He let her know that their plans were still on before hanging up and calling Mike and Ced.

The phone calls to Mike and Ced were merged calls, so all three of them were on a three-way call together.

"Damn, homie, I thought you were for sure done for," Mike said. "What the fuck going on?"

"Yeah, Ru, what's the word?" Ced asked.

"Look, I'ma slide on y'all tomorrow. We gonna have an emergency meeting. Gather everybody and let's meet at Riverside at 12:00 p.m.," he said.

Both Mike and Ced agreed before hanging up.

Joveezy drove to his house in Westville and parked in the garage next to the Hellcat Charger. He closed the garage door and took out the manilla envelope and placed it inside of the

Hellcat before letting Bonnie into the house and then entering himself.

Tango greeted him and Bonnie. So, Joveezy knew that the Feds didn't have a warrant to raid his home. "Fucking rookies." But that didn't mean that they weren't watching the house. If they were, he had a plan in motion, and a war was about to break out.

Joveezy headed to his bedroom to take out a new fit to wear tonight for his dinner date with Lisa. He looked at the time, and it was now 10:30 p.m.

He got in the shower and took a twenty-minute shower before getting dressed and driving his Charger to Lisa's house.

When he arrived at Lisa's, it was 11:20 p.m.

He took the spare key from the flowerpot and entered the home. Lisa was in the living room, sitting on the couch, sipping on a glass of white wine.

She looked up at Joveezy with a smile on her face and got up to embrace him with a long and deep kiss.

"Damn, Daddy, what happened, and why you ain't answer your phone all day?" she asked Joveezy.

"I got pulled over and taken in for questioning by some federal agents," he replied.

Lisa looked at Joveezy with a concerned look on her face. "So, what happened, bae? What did they say? What are they tryna do to you?"

"They don't have nothing on me, baby. So, they had to let me go, but something ain't right about how they just rolled up on me. Plus, they followed me from the house in West Willow."

"What you man they followed you? Did they raid the house?" Lisa asked.

"No, that's the funny part."

"So, what all did they ask?"

"They got to asking me questions about Ced, Beno, Mouse, and about the businesses," he said.

"And what did you say?"

"Nothing besides I got money from a bank as a loan and that I would like to have my attorney present. The whole time they were talking, I was quiet and ignoring those suckas. They were pissed," he replied, laughing.

"Baby, that shit ain't funny. I cannot afford to lose you. It would kill me inside to know I would lose you. Do they know you got the money from me and that I helped you get to where you are now?" Lisa questioned.

"Naw, love. Why would I bring you into the mess besi…"

Lisa cut him off. "Bae, I'ma legit woman with millions, and you my man. If me being your alibi is what can keep them Feds off your back, then so be it. I'ma reach out to some of my resources tomorrow and get this shit figured out. For now, let's just have a good time and take your mind off of things just for the time being.

'Okay, sweetheart. Let's go out," Joveezy said, giving Lisa a kiss, as they headed out the door.

They both got into the Mercedes truck. But before they pulled off, Joveezy went to the Charger, grabbed the manilla envelope, got back into the Mercedes truck, and pulled away from the house.

As he pulled away from the home, Joveezy looked into the rearview mirror, making sure no other cars followed. When no car followed, he eased up a little.

Chapter 10

The late-night restaurant was packed, and the scene was lively. The dim lighting gave off a radiant but laidback vibe that set the mood just right. The waitress led Joveezy and Lisa to their table and gave them menus to look over.

Joveezy and Lisa talked amongst themselves before their waitress came back to take their orders.

Lisa ordered lobster and crab legs with a side of greens fried in a little olive oil and pieces of bacon. Joveezy ordered a side of crab legs, fried jumbo shrimp, tilapia, and extra buttery rice with a hint of lemon pepper, a pinch of seasoning salt, and cayenne pepper, drizzled in honey.

Joveezy and Lisa ate their meal and were replenished. They talked about vacation trips they would take in the upcoming month or two. After sitting at the table for another ten minutes or so, the waitress brought them the check, and Joveezy paid the bill, and they both left hand in hand, happy and full.

"So, where you tryna go next, sweetheart?" Joveezy asked Lisa.

"I'm tryna go home and just lay back wit' you tonight, bae," Lisa replied.

"Are you sure that's what you want? It's all about you tonight."

"Yeah, I'm sure, Daddy. I rather be up under you all day and night. Plus, you owe me a week of just us two. Me, you, and no one else," she said.

"Aight, I'm down for that, baby," Joveezy agreed, kissing Lisa on the lips.

They got into the car and headed home to Lisa's place. By the time they arrived, it was a quarter past one in the morning.

Joveezy parked the car in the garage. Lisa headed into the house with Joveezy in tow with the manilla envelope in his hand.

"Bae, what's that you got?" Lisa asked, eyeing the envelope.

"This is something that came across my hands a couple days ago," he responded. "I need to look into the matter, but it's not that important."

He laid the manilla envelope down inside the dresser drawer in their bedroom before getting undressed to take a shower.

The shower was much needed after a long day. As soon as the water hit his body, he felt calmer and more refreshed.

His mind was distracted, as Lisa snuck into the shower with him. She snapped him out of his daze when she started rubbing and kissing on his neck and back.

He turned around to embrace her with a kiss and then planted light kisses on her chest until he reached her breasts. Lisa's chest rose and fell heavily with a rush of sexual rage, but she kept herself under control.

Joveezy ran his tongue over one of her breasts before taking a nipple into his mouth.

"Oohhh, shitt, bae," Lisa moaned.

Joveezy went to the next nipple and did the same, sending Lisa over the edge just a little.

"Oh, yes. Yes, that feels so good," she moaned.

He let her nipple fall out of his mouth and put one of her feet up on the tub for support and dropped down to his knees and devoured her sweet juices.

"Uummm ummm. Yes, Daddy, suck that pussy just like that," she cried out. She grabbed the back of his head and started grinding her pussy into his face. "Oohh, shit, yesss. Yess, Daddy. Fuck, I'm bout to cum."

Joveezy stuck two fingers into Lisa's pussy and fingerfucked her, as he sucked on her clit.

Lisa screamed, "Fuck, Daddy. There it is. I'm cumming."

He licked and sucked up all of the sweet juices her fruit had to offer until she started to get weak in the knees. He got up and turned Lisa around. He grabbed her and bent her over, as she placed her hands on the shower wall and rubbed the head of his dick in between her lips before inserting his dick into her with a hard thrust.

"Uuugghhh uuugghh. Fuucckkk, yesss, Daddy. Tear this pussy up. Mmm," Lisa moaned before cumming a second time.

The feel of Lisa's walls tightening around his dick made Joveezy start to release his load deep inside her.

They finished up their shower together and headed to the bedroom for round two and fucked until the crack of dawn started to peak.

Chapter 11

Lacey went to the bank and withdrew two hundred and fifty thousand dollars from her account. The plans she had with the money were pricey but well worth it.

She put the money in the trunk of her Porsche and drove across town to the westside of Detroit until she reached Joy Road. Like the eastside, this part of the city was overrun by gangs, and drugs always ran rampant. The neighborhoods and houses were nice, but the criminal activity always thrived, The kids were lingering on the streets, some enjoying the beautiful summer afternoon, other conducting their illicit business.

Lacey was all too familiar with this part of town. She was raised here and had more family over on the westside than the east. Some of her uncles and cousins ran with some of the most vicious gangs around and were major players in the dope game. The hustle and bustle of Detroit's drug industry was why the city alone was a plug city and so diverse in culture and mixed races. She took advantage of the hustle the streets of Detroit had to offer, and it became more and more of a financial playground for her.

She cruised in her Porsche, looking and feeling like a true royal boss woman. Dee-Dee was her companion and number one shadow. She was like a lioness lying in wait for prey and watching everything.

Lacey's eyes were on every movement and activity, as she cruised up Piedmont Street. The tints on the Porsche made it hard to see in but easy to see out of. She watched as the car turned heads, some looking in awe and amazement at the Porsche cruising through their neighborhood.

Lacey cruised a few more blocks, and then she came to a shop in front of a two-story, white house with black trimming on Piedmont Street. The house had a small, open front yard with a driveway that led to a fenced in backyard and one car garage.

On the porch sat four young niggas who looked to be between the ages of sixteen and nineteen years old. Upon her arrival, they got up, ready for an unexpected surprise.

Lacey shut off the car and looked at the house with the young goons who were now standing up, mean mugging the car. She and Dee-Dee noticed that they were armed.

"This is it," Lacey announced.

"Yeah, it looks like it," Dee-Dee replied.

They both stepped out of the car, Lacey clad in a pair of Balenciaga jeans, three-inch heels, and a white, off-shoulder, button up blouse.

She gazed up at the house, and the young men eased up a little but were still leery of the two women.

"Get the bag out the truck, so we can go handle this business."

Dee-Dee nodded and walked to the back of the car. She opened the trunk and removed a red and black Armani duffle bag. She closed the trunk and moved toward the house with Lacey following behind her.

The two of them weren't worried about trouble. Dee-Dee, in her white, Gucci, button-down shirt and tight-fitting, Dior blue jeans, along with her sexy but stone cold demeanor, concealed a Glock 10 under her shirt. She was a surgical demon with any weapon in her hand, a sharpshooter and a head busting killing machine.

As they approached the porch, the oldest of the four stepped to the top of it and caused Lacey and Dee-Dee to stop at the bottom of the stairs. He was tall and brown skinned with single braids.

"Damn, lovely ladies, what's up? Who y'all looking for?" he asked, looking them over and licking his lips.

"We here to see my uncle, Don," Lacey announced.

"Yo' uncle? Man, cut it out," he said, surprised.

"Nigga, cut what out? And who are you?!" she asked with a smug look on her face.

"I'm his son, Dontae. Hold on a minute. Let me go holla at him," he said, looking her over again before turning to head into the house.

Lacey and Dee-Dee waited patiently, as the younger goons eyed them awkwardly. Dee-Dee noticed a small, black, bubble shaped camera built in above the front door watching them from above. There were bars on the front window and the front door window, and the front door seemed thick with a black, iron gate in front of it. She also got a closer look at the heat they were toting – a Glock 40, a Mossberg, and a Glock 17.

A short moment later, Dontae came back and led Lacey and Dee-Dee into the house where they stepped into the hallway. On the right was a doorway leading to a living room, and on the left was the dining room. Next to the dining room were stairs, and at the stairs waiting was an armed man carrying a .45 caliber on his hip in a quick release holster.

"Your uncle is surprised by your visit and is happy to see you," the man informed, as he led them up the stairs. The hallway was narrow but spacey, as they made their way past two doors across from each other. Both doors were closed, but you could hear commotion coming from behind the closed doors. They came across two more doors. One was slightly ajar, and you could slightly make out surveillance monitors and one guard sitting behind the screens. The other door was wide open, and inside the room was a desk, a couch, and two chairs in front of the desk. The room seemed plain.

Behind the desk sat a heavyset man, hair cut low with a light fade. Tattoos were from his neck down, and he wore a grey Lacoste suit and a black button-down shirt that was slightly open.

The guard knocked on the door before entering with Lacey and Dee-Dee close behind. Upon their entrance, the man behind the desk looked up then stood to greet his visitors.

"Wow, you have grown up a lot, Lacey," Don said, stepping from behind his desk to embrace her with a long and gentle hug.

"Thank you, Uncle. I missed you," she said.

"What kept you away for so long? And what brings you by after all this time?"

"Well, for starters, it's a long story that we can talk about on a later note. But to make a long story short, I been through a lot as you probably heard."

"To be honest, this side of the family haven't heard too much ever since my sister, your mother, passed," he informed with a sad look on his face. "Have a seat. Let me know what's up."

"Look, Unc, I've been through some of the worst things imaginable. I've been kidnapped, raped, and drugged on numerous occ…"

"Wait, back up. You been through all that, niece? And we ain't know shit?" he asked with a puzzled and angered look on his face.

"Didn't nobody know because I didn't want to pain you all with the situation I been through."

"So, who did it, and how did you get away?" he asked.

"Let's just say a good friend got me out of a dire situation, and who did it or had part in it is why I am here now," she explained before placing the duffle bag of money on the table. "The nigga who fucked my world up before I made a comeback was my ex-fiancé, Dominic, and his partner in crime is Madame Charity. They used me and abused me like a dog, Unc," she said with tears forming in her eyes.

The memory of the shit she went through had her trembling all over. She was so upset and angry at herself for being so careless and blind to the betrayal that was brewing to destroy her and her life altogether.

"So, what do you ask of me, niece? Whatever your wish may be, I will surely grant it. You're family, and family will always have each other's back through thick and thin,' he said.

"There is two hundred and fifty thousand dollars in this duffle bag. I need Dominic's head delivered to me as proof of his departure from this life. And I need to find the whereabouts of Madame Charity and where she lays her head, even if I got to get to her family to draw her out," she said before pulling out her cellphone. "I want Madam Charity for myself."

Lacey pulled up a picture of Dominic and showed Don his target.

"Be careful, Unc. This nigga is dangerous as they come, and he keep some real hittas around him at all times. Even if you don't 'see his goons around, they will be close by and lurking," Lacey told Don.

"I got you, Lace. I'ma make sure we get on top of that, and I'ma do some research on Madame Charity for you," he said.

"Thank you. On to other matters, somebody got ahold of one of my plugs, and a bunch of stuff is missing. We don't know if it was an inside job or not, but I just want you to keep an ear to the streets about any person or persons who tryna move big product, jewelry included. The hit took place on the eastside."

"Damn, Lacey, you in deep, huh? Just be careful, and if you need extra muscle, just give me a call, and you know family gone go to war behind you. In the meantime, between time, I'ma keep my ears open and handle business for you," he assured.

"Yeah, I know. As a matter of fact, I got a proposition for you. When you get Dominic and find that bitch, Madam Charity, for me, I will bring you in on an operation I'm building, help you out as a token of my appreciation," she offered.

Don stood up, and Lacey and Dee-Dee did the same.

"We got a deal," Don said, extending his hand out to shake Lacey and Dee-Dee's hands.

"Deal," Lacey said with a smile of satisfaction on her face.

Lacey hadn't seen her uncle consistently since she was nine years old and then on and off after that until she was thirteen, right before her mother died. The stories she used to hear about her Uncle Don would scare the hell out of people who didn't know him, as if they were hearing nighttime horror storis. But she wasn't fazed. She knew that he would not hurt her or family – at least not those that hadn't deserve it.

She used to hear stories about her other uncles, aunties, and cousins that were also gruesome. But the stores and lifestyle Don lived outdid any torturous acts and devilish deeds that anyone could stand to tolerate.

Uncle Don was a master torturer. He brutalized his victims by cutting parts of their flesh off of their bodies, while they were still alive, and then he would pour gasoline on the wounds until his victim passed out from all the pain they were enduring. He would torture them for hours, using different methods and techniques, until he was finished playing with his prey. Some didn't make it through the torturing trial. But that didn't stop Don from committing such heinous acts even when they were dead.

Lacey and Dee-Dee left the room and walked out of the house. She passed Dee-Dee the keys and told her to drive, while she took a seat in the back to rest and think on all that had transpired in the last few days. She smiled to herself, knowing that she would soon have what she'd been seeking.

Now, it was just a matter of getting to the bottom of who got to her connect.

"Take me to see Keara," Lacey told Dee-Dee.

"Aw, shit," Dee-Dee said. "Girl, what you got up your sleeves now?"

"A whole bunch of tricks who love to put on shows. Since these niggas wanna perform, we gone give these streets a concert. It's bout time we leave a message in blood," Lacey said with a grin on her face and mischief on her mind.

Chapter 12

Keara was throwing the dick down her throat like it was a snack. Her plush and soft lips gripped around the nine-inch pipe she was chasing and gagging on. The moans in the room grew louder and louder. Keara cupped the young goon's nuts and sucked the soul out of his dick while jerking him off in a steady pace, her saliva coating every length of his dick.

He grabbed the back of her head, and his fist wrapped around her long, sandy brown locs, as her deep throating grew more intense. "Oohh, shit," he moaned. "Ssssssuck that dick just like that. Ooohh, damn, that feels so good!"

Keara quickly got off her knees and got undressed and was ready to be the sluttiest bitch with Sevyn for the rest of the evening.

Sevyn was a big time dope boy and shot caller for a squad of young hustlers trying to come up. He was twenty-five years old with the body of a gladiator. His arms were bulky, and his chest seemed powerful. His long dreads extended down his back, and his whole body was covered in tattoos from his neck to his stomach.

Sevyn bent Keara over her couch, closing her legs together, and put her in a face down position, holding her hands behind her back, her plump breasts dangling like mangos ready to be picked from a tree. He slowly thrust himself into her slippery, creamy, wet pussy, and she released a screaming moan, feeling the rigid penetration slam into her guts.

She broke free of his grasp and gripped the couch pillows tightly. "Ooohh, shit, Daddy," she cried. "Throw that dick deep inside me."

Sevyn's hand pushed down on the small of Keara's back so that there would be an arch into it. With his other hand, he grabbed a fistful of her hair and pulled until he could see the tip of her nose, as he fucked her from behind.

The dick inside of her felt like her insides were being ripped apart, as it turned inside of her with the intent to both torture and please every tight space of her walls. "Fuck me, Sevyn! Damn, you filling me up with that big dick! Oh, God. I can feel you all in my stomach!"

As the two of them were lost in the moments of pleasure and lust, Keara's cell phone started to ring. She chose to ignore whoever was calling because she was lost in the abyss of sex. The ringing stopped.

Keara threw her fat, jiggling, round ass back into the young goon's pelvis, taking his entire dick inside of her like a porn star. She closed her eyes and continued to moan loudly, as Sevyn went to work on the pussy.

They went from fucking doggy style to Keara on her back, her legs in the air and her knees damn near touching her ears, as Sevyn towered over her, slamming his hard dick into her pussy like a jackhammer. Keara proved she was flexible, now laying sideways on the couch, the dick punishing her like a drill.

Her phone rang again.

Keara looked up at Sevyn, who was lost in the pussy, handling his business like a real pro was supposed to. He didn't let unwanted distractions affect him. He was content and focused on his task.

"Just fuck this pussy, baby!" Keara cried out. She repositioned herself to take the dick while laying on her stomach froggy style, her ass cheeks spread wide open. Her sweet juices were dripping between her thighs, as Sevyn shoved his nine inches of solid wood into her.

Keara's walls were tightening around his dick. She felt herself about to cum again, but a sharp knock at the front door ruined the moment slightly. She wasn't expecting any company.

Sevyn raised up and stared at the door, his body glistening with sweat and a confused and frustrated look on his face. He looked at Keara for answers, but she was just as confused as he was, so she shrugged her shoulders.

The sharp banging at the front door continued and echoed through the house.

Sevyn got to his feet and reached for his pants. He didn't know what to expect. Maybe it was one of Keara's side niggas or jealous ex-boyfriend coming by unexpectedly to pay her a visit. As far as he knew, she claimed she was single. He hurried to put on his pants and grabbed his Luger 38 just in case. If it was an ex or current boyfriend about to be on bullshit, then he was ready to leave the nigga right where he stood and keep it moving.

Keara put on a long robe and went to answer the door, her face in a pissed off scowl, as she tied her robe closed. She peeked out the front door curtain, while Sevyn stood in the living room, shirtless, with his pistol in his hand and held down by his side.

"Bitch! What the fuck you doing, ho?" Keara screamed with excitement, opening the door

"Who dat, Ma?" Sevyn asked.

"Hey, Keara," Lacey smiled.

"Oh, my God. Look at you. Where you been?" Keara was shocked to see Lacey on this side of the city. Usually, she called her when she needed a favor.

"Bitch, can I come in?" Lacey asked. "I tried to call, but you didn't answer the phone."

Behind Lacey stood Dee-Dee like a shadow and her protector.

"Of course you can come in, cousin." Keara stepped to the side to allow the two to enter her house.

Lacey walked in and locked eyes on the young nigga who stood in the center of her relative's living room with the pistol in his hand. She didn't flinch but kept her cool, as did Dee-Dee, when they noticed Sevyn clutching.

Lacey shot a look at her cousin, and the look in her eyes spoke for themselves.

Keara read the expression and look on Lacey's face. "Bitch, please don't start. I was in here enjoying myself until you showed up unexpectedly, and I didn't plan on having company over this evening."

"I am here on business and need to talk to you," she looked at Sevyn, "in private. Please and thank you."

"Sevyn, baby, step out for a minute."

"You sure?" he asked.

"Yes, we good here. This is family."

Sevyn nodded, then he collected his things and walked toward the door.

Keara followed behind him, and before he made his exit, the two kissed passionately, while Lacey and Dee-Dee watched.

"Just know our session ain't over," Keara whispered in Sevyn's ear, causing him to smile.

"I already know, baby. I was enjoying that pussy for the time being."

"And I was enjoying that dick too. Sorry we had to stop our freak show, but I got to take care of this family matter."

"I ain't tripping. I understand how it is."

"Just so you know, this pussy ain't going nowhere."

Sevyn smiled again, and they tongue wrestled once more.

"Keara! Bitch, come on now. This shit important," Lacey chimed in.

"Aight, bitch. Damn!" Keara said playfully. "You do know you in my domain now, and you gotta be respectful."

'You got it, girl," Lacey laughed. "But come on. Shit need to be handled."

Keara said her goodbye to Sevyn and closed the door behind him. She turned around and took in Lacey's wardrobe for the first time and knew that her cousin was rolling in cash. She was playing in an untamed world of blood and mayhem, and Keara wanted to be in the center of it all too.

She put on her game face and walked to the dining room with Lacey and Dee-Dee following close behind her.

They took their places at the antique, round table positioned in the middle of the dining room.

"Aight, so, what's up, family?" Keara asked, looking at Lacey and Dee-Dee.

Keara knew Dee-Dee was a long-lost relative from Lacey's dad's side of the family. When Lacey's father, Sam, got killed by the police, Dee-Dee popped up out of nowhere and attended his funeral. Her Uncle Corey was the one who introduced the two right before Lacey's disappearance. When Lacey came back, the two were inseparable, and Lacey went nowhere without Dee-Dee. But the two of them here at Keara's house to handle business meant it was time to get serious because her assistance was needed.

"Well, first of all, there is a lot of shit in the mix that's going on, and I needed you to get back to the team. So, my question to you is are you in or out?" she asked Keara.

Keara looked at Lacey as if she was dumbfounded. "Fam, I don't even know why you coming at me like that. You know I'm down to get messy and stay with the bullshit," she said.

"Aight, so dig this. We got some shit in motion. Right now, I need you to dig into a bitch named Madame Charity and her whereabouts. This bitch is top priority along with my ex-Dominic. So, look around and ask trustworthy people you know and trust to keep business discreet. On another matter, ask some of your niggas you be messing around with if they know about any niggas who recently made a come up and sitting nicely. Some shit happened, and I need to find out who got down on one of my connects."

"Okay, so how soon do you need all of this done?" Keara asked.

"The sooner the better. I got two hundred and fifty thousand dollars to bring back any info and whereabouts about Madame Charity. No false information. This shit is important, Keara," Lacey stressed.

"I got you, Lace," said Keara.

Chapter 13

The meeting that was supposed to be held that day was one of the first that would both rock and shake up Joveezy's crew. So much was at stake. He promised Lisa that he would spend the week with her, so he had to make good on the promise while still taking care of business as well, which was the meeting with Ced, Mike, Beno, and Mouse along with other members of Joveezy's crew of goons.

That morning at 5:30 a.m., Joveezy woke up early and made a call to one of his friends, Cheryl, for a favor for Lisa. He had Cheryl schedule appointments for Lisa starting at 9:00 a.m. for her to get her hair and nails done. Then, at 11:30 a.m. she was to take a trip to the spa and at 1:00 p.m., a trip to the massage parlor to get rubbed down with oils and lotions. He wanted to keep Lisa busy and content so that he could get away and handle his business.

After he set up the appointments for Lisa and made the necessary payments, it was six thirty a.m. Lisa was still asleep, so he decided to get in the shower. When he got out, it was seven thirty a.m. He took care of his hygiene and picked out a casual fit for his meeting, something slight and not too formal. He dressed himself in a pair of black Chrome Heart jeans, a white Ferragamo belt with a gold Medusa head buckle, a white V-neck t-shirt, and a pair of mid-top white Jordans. To ice himself out and complement his wardrobe, he put on two gold Cuban links. One was a choker with crushed white diamonds, and the other chain had a rose gold cross with crushed diamonds. He also put on a pair of rose gold diamond encrusted screw back earrings and a gold Movado watch with one pointers in the face. The side arm he chose from a medium sized safe in the back of their closet with a holster to fit was a chrome Colt forty-five. It was custom made with red handles and black hearts engraved on the handles.

By seven fifty a.m., Lisa stared to wake up. Joveezy gave her a kiss on her soft, full lips and told her the plans he had made for her that day.

"Aww, Daddy, are you serious? All for me?" she said with a smile on her face.

"Yeah, baby. I know you need some special treatment, and it's all on me. That way, while you getting your relaxation time, I can run some errands."

"Thank you, Daddy, but I like how you still found a way to go handle business," she said with a sad look on her face. "You promised me the week."

"Baby, ain't nothing changed at all. I am still keeping that promise I made to you. It's just that ordeal with the Feds got my mind in a haze, and I need to address it, sweetheart. So please forgive me."

"All is forgiven, my love. Just as long as you still keep your word with me is all that matters, Daddy."

"I got you, sweetheart," he said, kissing her on the lips again." Now go get ready. Your first appointment starts at nine o'clock."

Lisa stretched and got out of bed and headed for the shower. Joveezy heard the sink cut on and after a few minutes, the shower cut on after hearing the bathroom door close.

He pulled out his cell phone and made a call to Ced.

"What up doe?" Ced answered the call.

"What's good, Slime?" Joveezy asked.

"What's da word, bro? I'm waiting on your next power move."

"Is everything set in motion for this meeting?"

"Yeah, I just got to the meet up also, so I could get everything settled. I called Beno, Mouse, and the rest of the counsel who needed to attend, so everyone is aware of the urgent gathering and where to link up at," Ced stated.

"Aight, make sure you have some of the homies working the block. Any suspicious cars just sitting and out of place needs to be reported back to one of us immediately and make sure to tell them not to approach them people or act out of character. Everyone should circle the block a couple times and park in various places. We don't need to draw attention and use the back door only."

"Aight, bool. Other than that, what's good with you, bro? Is everything bool on your end?"

"To be honest, Blood, shit ain't adding up, but we gon' figure it out. Right now, I'ma little on edge on how everything happened how it did," Joveezy confessed.

"I'm already knowing, Slime. I'm just as lost as you, but I kinda figured sooner or later, the spotlight would eventually shine brighter in our direction. I mean, look at us."

"Yeah, even when you cover your tracks, you still got people who cannot keep out of niggas' business. But aye, Ru, I'ma slide out dat way in a minute. I need to make a quick call right quick. Something just popped up."

"Aight, bro. I'ma bark at you when you get here," Ced said before ending the call.

Joveezy scrolled in his phone and found a name, Don, in his phone and hit the call button. On the second ring, Don picked up.

"Hello," said Don with sleep still in his voice.

"Aye, yo, this Jo. Bro, I got some serious shit on my hands. I need you," Joveezy said.

"Yeah, yeah. Um, what's up, Jo? Talk to me. What can I do for you?" Don asked. From the sound of his voice, he was stretching while yawning.

"Well, for starters, the Feds slid on me out of nowhere."

"Wait, wait, wait. Hold on there a minute," Don said, cutting Joveezy off. 'What you mean the Feds slid on you? When did this happen, and what did they ask? How long did they hold you for? And did they raid you or what?"

"No, they pulled me over, raided my truck, and took me in for questioning and let me go after hours of bullshit in which I didn't have time for. This happened yesterday, but I don't want to get into details over the phone. I need a favor is why I'm calling," Joveezy said.

"Yeah. Yeah, okay, my bad. What you need?"

"I need you to check my Trackhawk for a tracker and see if them pigs bugged my truck. If so, you know what to do. And later on, I'ma have you do some digging and research for me. It's important you dig deep. I'ma hit you up and find out what you got for me later on today."

"Okay. Now we talking my line of work. I got you," Don said with eagerness in his voice.

"Aight, Don. I appreciate you, bruh. I'ma make sure I compensate you as soon as I hang up and send you the research I need you to dig up," he said.

"Okay, cool, man. I'ma get around to doing that as soon as you send me what you want me to look into."

"Bet dat up," Joveezy said before ending the call.

Joveezy used a Text Now number to send the two Federal agents' names to Don and let him know that he needed all of the information on them that would be useful. And he meant everything. After sending the message, Joveezy deleted the app and wired Don twenty-five thousand dollars to his secured account under business transactions. He went to grab the manilla envelope and resumed looking through the photos. After looking through the majority of the photos, he came across a couple of photos that caught his eye. One of the photos contained the federal agent, Dom, and his partner. They were in plain clothes, talking to some Mexicans at an airport. After seeing this, he took a photo on his phone and sent it to Don with a message. "This is those two ducks I was inquiring about."

Don texted back. "Checking the pond now and thank you for the delivery. Just received the package and deleting this text."

Joveezy did the same and continued looking through the photos. Another photo contained the same Mexican talking to a familiar face that he knew very well.

Joveezy heard the shower cut off, and he hurried to put the photos back into the envelope. Lisa came into the bedroom with a towel wrapped around her wet hair and nothing covering her nakedness.

"What's wrong, Daddy? You look upset," she said, noticing the concerned and bothered look on his face.

"I'm alright, baby. I just thought about something that had me in thought for a moment."

"Are you sure? Or does it have something to do with that envelope you holding?" she inquired.

"To be honest, Lisa, it has a little to do with this envelope and with what happened yesterday. But it ain't nothing to stress too much about."

"Are you sure, my love? Because I can't tell if there's anything you need me to do. You know I am here for you all the way to the end and back."

"And I know it," he said, smiling. He got off the bed, walked over to her, and embraced her with a kiss, squeezing her ass cheeks. "But I got this under control. Now, get dress ed, sweetheart, so we can get ready to head out."

By the time Lisa got dressed and ready, it was getting nearer to 8:30 a.m. She put on white Juicy Couture shorts with a pink and white Gucci shirt and pink and white Air Maxes to match. She also put on a white pearl necklace and earrings along with a custom plain jane Rolex made with a white diamond set as the dial on the watch.

As she was finishing up with touching herself up and putting her hair up, Joveezy took the time to look up the address he found in the manilla envelope with the photos. The address led back to a cemetery in Detroit.

"I'm ready, Daddy," Lisa said, snapping Joveezy out of deep thought.

"Aight, baby. Let your day of relaxation and special treatment begin, all at my expense." He grabbed her hand in his, and as they headed out the house, he tucked the address in the envelope.

Joveezy took Lisa to the hair and nail salon first. Cheryl pulled up at the same time as they did in a black Audi S4 rebuilt for speed to outrun almost anything, and the car was bulletproof with run flat wheels. Joveezy let Lisa know that Cheryl would act as her chauffer until her appointments were over and that they would meet up at a restaurant in downtown Ann Arbor for brunch. Although Lisa wasn't too happy about the ordeal, she was acceptant of the fact. She enjoyed Cheryl's company and knew she would be in good health and hands. Joveezy gave Lisa a long and deep kiss and headed on his way.

Chapter 14

The Greens were a bunch of apartments that set in sections of three buildings with four connecting apartments. Each building had their own parking spaces, affordable prices, and section eight housing. Kids were out, playing everywhere, and the women were out, showing off in the tightest booty shorts and smallest t-shirts they could find. Most of them were probably wearing their children's t-shirts. Some of the young hustlas, who Joveezy recognized as some of his runners, were posted, watching the activity, and some were either shooting dice, showing off their cars, or engaged in a flirtatious conversation with a pretty vixen that walked past.

Joveezy parked his cherry red G-Wagon at a liquor store right across the street from the apartment complex and went inside. As the door closed, he turned and looked out the store door to see if any suspicious vehicles were following him or seemed out of place. Once satisfied, he left back out and crossed the street to the apartments that were away from the main streets and entered the back of one of the apartments that set off to the side.

The apartment was small yet spacious but had even more space since the walls were knocked out to access the next-door apartment as well, which turned the two apartments into one double. Cedarwood slider doors separated the two apartments. Both apartments still had its original looks and setups with two of each now, and upstairs, both apartments had three bedrooms apiece, now making it six bedrooms.

One apartment's living room was turned into a game room with two blackjack tables, a poker table, and a craps' table. The dining room was turned into a conference room with a black and gold glass top table to seat fifteen people. There was a personal bar built into the wall with four shelves of various liquor, a medium refrigerator, and ice machine. The air was filled with Cuban cigar smoke, and the apartment was lively with conversation. All that attended the meeting in accordance were the only ones who knew about the apartments. In total, there were eight people in attendance – Ced, Mike, Beno, Mouse, Nico, Craig, Chris, and Joveezy himself.

Everyone greeted Joveezy with a nod, and those who had a glass in their hands raised it to salute him. He greeted everyone back and headed to pour himself a glass of Hennessy before taking his place at the head of the table. Once seated, everyone got quiet and focused their attention on him. He laid the manilla envelope on the table before taking a swig from his glass.

"Look, gentlemen," Joveezy began after clearing his throat, "I called this meeting because we got a major situation some of us may know about that needs to be addressed and taken very seriously, and for those that don't know, all is about to be told to you now. To get straight to the point, Feds picked me up yesterday as I was leaving my crib in West Willow, claiming they been investigating us for about a month, which isn't enough time for them to snatch me up how they did. Plus, they didn't raid my house, so shit not adding up. They had enough info on us to spook me though. They know about my business and questioned how I came across the money to be able to start these chains of businesses, but further investigation into that came back legit, thanks to my woman. But here's where it gets interesting. They know about you, Beno, and how you got ties with the 'migos and suspects you distribute for the Cartel, said they been watching you for some time now."

Beno smacked his lips. “Man, fuck them suckas. If they know that much, why they ain’t slide yet?” he questioned.

“Good question,” Joveezy agreed, “Somebody talking to the Feds. We can determine who today in these photos I got, so we gone find out who da rat is. Furthermore, they know too much about our personal and close circle and how long we been knowing each other. Yeah, they mentioned you too, Ced. They know you my righthand and shadow and suspects you calling shots on my behalf. But that’s all they got so far on that topic.”

“Fuck, so they got it all figured out, huh?” Ced said, laughing. “So, what’s next? What we gone do now?”

“Well, I’ma get to that because here’s where shit gets real,” he said, spilling out the photos from the manilla envelope and separating them out for everyone to see. “These photos came from that demonstration that took place a few days ago. I know the chick in the photo who know the Italians. That’s my relative, Lacey. What she got to do with them, I don’t know….”

“Damn, Blood,” said Beno, pointing to a photo. “That’s one of our cocaine connects. His name is Chino. We been dealing with him for a minute now.”

“Yeah, that’s the one I met in Barbados on a party yacht, and he became our supplier. Them peoples our guy, Chino, is meeting up wit’ in that photo is them federal agents who took me in for questioning. So, I’m thinking our guy, Chino, been dealing with the Feds and has been their informant for some time now,” Joveezy determined.

“Okay, so how do the rest of these people tie back in to us? And what does our connect got to do with them people in the other photos?” asked Ced.

‘I don’t know,” admitted Joveezy, “but something still missing and ain’t adding up. Like was Chino setting me up from the first day we met? Because now that I think about it, shit was too coincidental. He was too eager to let me know he was a supplier and put me on, and I took the bait on thirsty shit. Which gave the Feds enough time to find out about me and been building a case on us for years and not just a month now. It makes sense."

"Aye, check dis out," said Mouse, holding up one of the photos in his hand. "Ain't that yo' whip, Beno, leaving the 'migo's crib?"

In the photo was a money green SRT8 Dodge Challenger with black Forges. The window was down, so you could barely just make out Beno's face in the photo from the angle it was taken from. He was talking to the Mexican, Chino, and exchanged three duffle bags in total.

"What the fuck?!" said Beno, lost after seeing the photo. "I don't understand how the fuck they caught me slippin'."

"Man, fuck dat. What's we gon' do?" Ced asked Joveezy.

"Well, here's my plan. We start finding out who else could be an informant. It's obvious Chino been setting us up, so we need to play Chino a visit and knock him out the way because he bogus, so we must eliminate the threat first and foremost. Just know there is going to be a war with his cartel crew, The Loko Cartel. So, put all soldiers on alert and make sure they ready for whatever. Also, I got someone digging into our federal agents. Once I get more intel on them, we pushing that drill to them too and anyone else who stands in our way."

"Fuck it! We gotta do what we got to do," said Mike. "I know for a fact shit gone hit da fan if we body one of them federal fucks, and it's gonna be hell to pay. Plus, the news gonna go crazy. Shiiddd, they may fuck around and get CIA invoiced in the ordeal – government, president, army, and coast…"

"Man, fuck dem. They can bring da heat," Chris said, cutting off Mike. "We already on the radar, and once the Feds on to you, indictments and everything else is also in the making. I don't know bout y'all, but I ain't goin' out like no sucka. I rather die than go to prison. What about yo' people in da photos doe, Jo? What we gone do about her?"

"I don't 'know yet," Joveezy said. "As of now, all I know is she connected too and the Feds on to her as well."

"So, are you going to let her know?" Chris asked.

"Naw, let's see how it plays out on her end. I'm thinking she in the dark and don't know she being watched by the Feds, or she may be involved. Who knows? But I do know she know those Italians we hit, and I don't want her to know we hit 'em," Joveezy said. "In the meantime, let's put matters into effect starting with Chino. And in the next twenty-four hours or so, I shall have the intel I need on them agents," he continued. "Until then, this meeting of counsel is adjourned. Ced, let me holla at you."

"What's the word, bro?" Ced asked with a puzzled look on his face.

Joveezy pulled the piece of paper out of his pocket that had the address of the cemetery written on it with the message. "This was inside the manilla envelope with them photos. I looked up the address, and it came back to a cemetery in Detroit. The message says, 'under the moonlight, you will find my heart and soul.' And that's all it says. I am still puzzled on the message. I'm starting to think it's a clue though. What you think?" he asked Ced.

Ced took a few seconds to ponder on the message before he answered. "To be honest, I think we should check out that location. It's definitely a clue to something important of course, especially since it says under the moonlight, meaning the moonlight is the key to what it reflects on and exposes what is hidden in the dark. It's like that phrase, 'What's in the dark will eventually come to light.' So, I assume the moonlight will shine on a spot in which will lead us to this heart and soul in the cemetery. What we will find is the question. Although I got a feeling it's dealing with a corpse."

"Aight, I'ma slide wit' you."

"Fasho. In da meantime, I need to go meet up with Lacey. I'ma get up with you later. And I should have that information on them federal agents too. Make sure you round up all the hittas in the next few days, so we can make that move on Chino and his men."

"Without a doubt, I'ma get to it."

"Aight, Blood," said Joveezy before heading out the back of the apartment and heading back to his truck.

He sat in his truck for a couple minutes to reflect on today's meetings and all that transpired in the last week. He was both excited but frustrated because he knew that with success came failure and vice versa. But the failures were no exceptions and brought consequences of unwanted problems. And he had a choice to make – sacrifice everything or fight. He knew what he had to do, and the latter was mandatory. He didn't build a foundation to start a legacy for nothing. He refused to give it all up due to some punk ass federal agents and snitches trying to rain on his parade. He started up his truck with a devilish grin on his face and proceeded to meet up with Lisa in downtown Ann Arbor.

Chapter 15

After the drive back home from Keara's house, Lacey was exhausted. Night was at its peak when she arrived at her and Nightmare's house, which was quiet. She moved around the house to see where everyone was at, including Nightmare, and no one was in sight. She pulled out her cell phone and called him but got no answer.

Lacey got undressed and headed to the shower to wash away today's unrest, and as she got in the shower, her cell phone rang. She looked at the caller ID and smacked her lips before answering.

"What the fuck you calling me for, Dominic, you punk ass nigga?" she asked with anger resonating from her voice.

Dominic said nothing, only breathed into the phone before he hung up.

Lacey went into her bedroom and got dressed to find Dee-Dee. She was in the kitchen, making a turkey, bacon, and cheese sandwich with lettuce, tomatoes, onions, and honey mustard. Dee-Dee looked up and noticed the frustrated and angry expression on Lacey's face.

"What's up, Lace?" questioned Dee-Dee.

"Well, for starters, ain't it strange nobody here? And two, Dominic keeps calling my phone."

"Well, block his number, girl. You were supposed to do that in the first place, and everybody probably out stealing," she replied, laughing.

"Yeah, well, I ain't want to give him the satisfaction, especially since he needs to be on my radar," Lacey explained. "And usually, Nightmare leaves guards here. That's mandatory he do that."

"You definitely right. Did you check the security room to see it they in there? They probably holding a meeting."

"No, I didn't check the barn. I was in the shower, but I'ma go check it out."

"Okay, I'ma come with you," Dee-Dee said, biting into her sandwich.

Lacey and Dee-Dee left the house through the back door and the backyard. The backyard had acres of land with lots of room for a herd of horses to run and roam as well as graze on the pasture. A huge, two-story barn was located about a hundred paces from the ranch style house. Five fenced in spaces surrounded the barn with colts and their mothers to tend to them, and two spaces were empty to train horses in. Dee-Dee entered the barn first then Lacey. As they walked in the barn, it was dark, and the horses were jittery and uneasy.

"Why the fuck is it so dark in here?" asked Dee-Dee, flicking the light switch on.

The lights came on, illuminating the barn. There were twenty stalls, ten on each side. Majority of the stalls held horses, but four didn't. The first stall was empty except for a few hay bales and a set of stairs leading up to the second floor of the barn. Lacey made her way up the stairs with Dee-Dee behind her. On the third step from the landing, Lacey stopped. Dee-Dee bumped into her.

"Damn, bitch, why you stopped?" asked Dee-Dee, a little irritated.

Lacey didn't say anything, just stood there, frozen in place, before walking up toward the top landing. Dee-Dee looked past Lacey and saw what she was staring at. Blood ran down the wooden stairs with a body barely visible at the top landing. Dee-Dee immediately unholstered her Glock 10 and moved ahead of Lacey. They both moved at a slow pace, and Dee-Dee hit the light switch at the top of the stairs. The lights came on, and Dee-Dee immediately scanned the upstairs barn. The upstairs barn had walls, so you couldn't look down into the stalls. It was refurnished into an office space and weapons cache for their security with bunk beds that lined the walls, twenty-two bunk beds in total. Eight more bodies lay scattered. Bullet holes riddled the barn walls. Lacey quickly snatched up an AR-15 lying next to one of the dead security guards. She checked the magazine to make sure it still had bullets and one in the chamber. Satisfied, she continued to look around in disbelief and astonishment at the bloody scene before them. She tapped Dee-Dee on the shoulder and pointed to a room. The door was halfway open with a dead security guard sitting against the wall opposite the door. He was slumped with his head on his chest.

Dee-Dee stood to the other side of the door with Lacey standing close behind her. Dee-Dee peeked into the room, but it was too dark to see in except for a light source coming from a TV screen. They listened for a few seconds before Dee-Dee pushed the door open and got down on one knee, ready to shot anyone that moved. She realize that no one was in the room, but three more dead security guards lay on top of the control's panel which was located in the center of the security room with stools built to the floor, while the other two were sprawled on the floor with their faces and chests riddled with bullet holes.

Lacey went to the security cameras and was pissed by what she saw. There were ten TV screens, five on both sides of the room, mounted on the walls, each showing video footage of all areas throughout the whole estate. Nine of the TV screens were shot up and no longer useable. The other one was on, and the camera was pointed at the door in which the room lights flickered. On the door was an arrow pointed to the right that looked like it was painted in blood by the color of it and how it ran down the door.

"Oh, my God," said Dee-Dee, standing next to Lacey.

Lacey went to the control panels, pulling the dead security dude off the controls with Dee-Dee's help. Some parts of the controls were damaged from the bullets that pierced it. Lacey found the controls that controlled the movement of the camera, and she moved the camera to the right, and as she moved the camera, she stopped on what the culprit wanted her to see. She screamed and broke down into tears.

"Nooo," she yelled. "Why would they do this?"

Dee-Dee grabbed her and hugged her.

Lacey got up and ran down the stairs at breakneck speed.

"Lacey, wait up, where you going?" Dee-Dee yelled, running behind her.

Lacey didn't respond. She knew exactly where the room with the body was. She ran to the seventh stall on the right side of the barn. The stall was empty except for another dead security guard and a cellar door that led to a set of concrete stairs. She went down the stairs and came into a long corridor with a bunch of rooms. There were all sorts of rooms with desks and some that looked like holding cells. Dee-Dee and Lacey noticed more bodies that they didn't recognize because they were not one of theirs. These men had on full body armor, black and gray camouflage, and night vision head gear. Their weapons were military grade weapons with silencers and so were their gear. At least five men lay dead in the hallway and one more at the end of the hallway.

Lacey and Dee-Dee took caution and looked into each room as they walked by, even sweeping the room whose doors were wide open, to make sure no one was hiding in them. Once they cleared the rooms, they went to the end of the hall. At the end of the hall to the left was another hallway that was shorter than the main hallway. More bodies of unknown people lay in the hallway amongst their own. This time, Dee-Dee and Lacey couldn't believe their eyes. Laying on his back with two bullet holes in his skull and his throat slit ear to ear was Nightmare's cousin, Menace.

Lacey stepped over the body and went to the door he was laying in front of and opened it. She walked into the room, saw what she saw on the camera, and ran to the body and hugged it with tears of pain and anger. She stepped back with blood now all over the side of her face, hair, and clothing and looked at Nightmare. He was hung on the wall with flat head screwdrivers embedded into the palm of each hand. His shoes were removed, and his feet were laid on top of each other with a flat head screwdriver ran through them. His body was hung up as if he were Jesus nailed to the cross. His eyes were gouged out, and his mouth was cut open to give him a Joker smile and sewed up to keep his mouth from hanging open. A metal pole was rammed through the wall between his legs and up against his nuts to keep him hoisted up. Whoever did the work took their time and pleasure to make their art presentable.

"Who would do something like this?" Dee-Dee asked with a ghostly look on her face.

"I know who would do this," Lacey sobbed. 'The same nigga who been tryna kill me, but how the fuck he know where I'm at is the question. It don't make sense unless he been following us or got someone on the inside that was under our noses the whole time."

"I don't know, but we ain't safe here, Lacey. We gotta go now," Dee-Dee insisted.

"Okay, I need to get some shit first. Go grab video footage from the security room and call the police and report this."

"Kay, I'ma make a anonymous call, and I'ma be honest with you. The video tapes are gone. That's the first thing I saw was missing from the security room," Dee-Dee admitted.

"Okay," Lacey said, heading out. "Let's go."

They headed out of the room and back upstairs to the barn before Lacey's phone started ringing again.

"Hello?" she answered without looking to see who was calling.

"You like my aftermath, sweetie?" asked a familiar voice.

"How did you get my number, bitch?" Lacey asked, looking at Dee-Dee, who was putting her ear next to Lacey's, trying to listen in on the call.

"It doesn't matter. What matter is you took something from me, and now, I will take everything you love dearest and closest to you. There is nowhere you can run or hide, sweetie," the caller said before hanging up the phone.

"Who was that bitch?" Dee-Dee asked.

Lacey looked at Dee-Dee with a horrified look on her face and replied, "Madame Charity."

As they came out of the barn and into the night, they heard several cars pull up front, screeching to a halt, and car doors slam. Voices of men could be heard, as Lacey and Dee-Dee ran around on the side of the barn to where a pickup truck attached to a house trailer sat. The truck door was unlocked, and they got inside. Lacey found the keys above her head in the visor. She started up the truck but kept the headlights off, as she eased the truck around the back of the barn before gunning it to the main road. Gunshots could be heard pinging of the truck's trailer, as they headed into the night.

Chapter 16

The nighttime trip to Detroit was a cool one, and the summer breeze was welcoming to Joveezy. It was twelve thirty when he, Ced, Bank, Rawdy, and Lil Loko made their way from Ypsilanti to Detroit. The drive was a quiet one for the most part. Everyone rode in Joveezy's G-Wagon, content on tonight's mission. They were toting 9mms, Sig Sauers, Desert Eagles, and three Glock 40s with buttons on the back and thirty-round extended clips. Lil Durk's *When I'm Lonely* blared out of the 2,800-watt sound system installed in the truck.

Going into the cemetery, none of them knew what or who would be waiting on them. Things were already krazy as it was. Earlier that morning, Don called Joveezy with information quicker than he anticipated, but with the happy and geeked up tone in Don's voice at his discovery, Joveezy was eager to hear what Don had found out. And what he learned from Don put a smile on his face. The two federal agents created bogus investigations and sting operations on Joveezy and his crew, meaning the Feds were as crooked as they come, which was rarely heard of in this line of work. There were no visible warrants or signed affidavits by a judge to conduct or authorize their investigation. That led Joveezy to believe that someone, and not just the Mexican connect, was involved. He'd already figured that, but why were they after him and for what?

Don couldn't find out who the true mole was but let him know about the Mexicans and other familiar faces Joveezy already knew of by the photos he'd seen. Whoever the other persons of interest were, they had to be secretly meeting the Feds in person and feeding loads of shit to them, and whoever the other person or persons were, they wanted out of the picture sooner than later. With this newfound information, Joveezy had a new tactic, and that was to get the information he needed to get ahold of the two federal agents and seek out who put the Feds on him.

Joveezy was snapped back to reality by the sound of Ced's voice talking to him over his thoughts and the music playing. He turned the radio down a few notches.

"What's up?" Joveezy asked.

"I asked if you were good, bro. By the looks of it, you seem like you were in deep thought, so what's on your mind?"

"I ain't gone lie, bro. A lot been on my mind, one being what we gone find at the cemetery and two, the shit with the Feds. To be real with you, I'm just ready to get all this shit off my back. The one thing I hate the most is looking over my shoulders for the enemy, wondering if and when they gone strike. But I know that's what come with the game, and I am also smart enough to know that having enemies and tryna make money put a stipulation in shit, causing unnecessary setbacks and untimely dilemmas. Like they say, you can't beef *and* get money. Wars *cost* money."

"Yeah, you right about all that, Jo, and the good thing 'bout all this is we got the money to do whatever," Ced said.

"With no doubt, we do," Joveezy agreed, laughing.

Joveezy's truck pulled off of the State Fair freeway on the eastside 7 Mile of Detroit and pulled into a BP gas station. When he pulled up, a few young hustlers were out trying to make a come up. Other than that, the activity at the gas station was at a low. He got out of the G-Wagon with lil Loke and Banks in tow as security, as he entered the store. Ced was already at the pump, waiting to feed the gas through the gas tank. Twenty minutes later, they arrived at the cemetery that the address led them to.

The cemetery was one of the more well-known cemeteries on Detroit's eastside. A lot of teenagers were drawn to it and adopted it as their refuge some of the time. The Greenwood Cemetery was lined with row after row of plots, trees, and headstones of all sorts, and the moon was at its brightest tonight, casting an illuminating spell over the graveyard's resting grounds.

Joveezy drove in the cemetery, cruising at a slow pace, taking in the scenery and allowing the moonlight to point him in the right direction. Eventually, they came to an area toward the back middle area of the cemetery where an old and run down crypt still stood. He parked the truck, and everyone got out. Ced made his way to a row of headstones closest to the crypt and began to look at the graves, trying to decide which one the moonlight gave its source of light to the most. When Ced found the spot, he called Joveezy over.

"Y'all hang back and keep an eye out," Joveezy told his hittas.

Joveezy walked to the gravesite where Ced was standing and pointing at. The headstone read: "Here lies Earnest Goodwill Rodriquez (1963-2010). Under the moonlight, the stars shine brightest on you, and your heart will never be soulless." On the tombstone, the moonlight hit a metal emblem of a Phoenix bird, which shone bright like a diamond.

"This got to be the place," Joveezy said.

"Hell yeah, this got to be it," Ced replied while gazing up at the moon. "The moon ain't shining its grill nowhere else like it is here."

"Aight then. Let's get the shovels and get to work." Joveezy headed back to the truck and told Banks and Rawdy to help him grab the shovels and dig up the grave. "Lil Loke, you fall back. I need your eyes, goon," he told him.

"I got you, big homie."

Joveezy, Banks, and Rawdy headed back to the grave, and Joveezy handed one of the two shovels he held to Ced, and they began to dig.

The four of them dug for nearly two and a half hours before they hit something hard. Banks used his hands to brush some of the remaining dirt, revealing a white, marble top casket. As he continued to brush off the rest of the dirt with the help of Rawdy, the casket soon came into clearer view. It was a white, marble, custom made casket with gold trimming. On the casket's lid lay a carving of a red Phoenix with gold and green tripped flames surrounding it.

Joveezy told everyone to get out of the grave and used his shovel to pry open the casket. When the casket's lid finally gave way and popped open, dust rushed out and settled in the air. The pungent, foul smell of long sealed coffin became apparent. It was literally picked clean to the bone over the years by beetles and other nightcrawlers, which crawled over the corpse from the faint light of the moon. The skull of the corpse still had a full head of gray, long, flowing hair attached. The skeleton was dressed in a fine, custom Louis suit with the initials E.G.R. stitched in gold thread on the left breast pocket of the red suit. The suit's collar and cuffs were also gold in color with red, ruby cufflinks. A gold chain rested around the neck of the corpse with a gold Phoenix medallion decorated in red rubies covering the medallion with green diamonds for the eyes of the Phoenix. In the corpse's clutched, skeleton, boney hand was a red cane with a gold Phoenix head at the top, and on the base of the cane, going down the length, it read, "The king shall live for eternity." One of the fingers wore a gold ring with the initials E.G.R., while the rest of his fingers had diamond rings on them.

"What you find down there, bro?" asked Ced.

"Nothing yet, but this nigga, whoever he is, must've been important, and they made sure to bury him like he was royalty in hella jewelry," Joveezy told Ced.

Still looking at the corpse, Joveezy noticed something sticking out of its gold-plated mouth. He grabbed it and noticed that it was rolled up like a scroll. He unrolled it carefully and read the paper. On the paper, it read, "Half is here; the other half is there. What's inside will lead you farther but near." He passed the note up to Ced.

"Man, what the fuck's up with all these riddles? This shit like the scene from *Tomb Raiders* or something," Joveezy said.

Ced laughed. "Yeah, whoever these clues was meant for must be into that type of shit. But I hope this ain't what we came for and that bullshit jewelry he wearing."

"Naw, the note say half is here. I'ma keep looking."

Joveezy rolled the corpse on its side carefully to look underneath it. The corpse was cold and stiff but started to break down like dust in some places of the skull and bones when he moved it. He found nothing, so he gently laid the corpse down on its back and pulled out his cell phone to use the flashlight to look around the inside of the casket. After a couple of minutes, he spotted, in the top corner of the casket, that part of the material was not stitched up all the way, leading to a sort of flap, so he began to pull at it, and it started to peel away like a banana.

As the fabric began to pull away more and more, he began to quickly see the rest of the fabric as the contents began dropping into the casket. He could hear Ced, Banks, and Rawdy whistle at the findings of the hidden wall's treasure. Ced jumped down into the pit with Joveezy, and they both began to examine the contents of the packages. Most of the packages contained a medium sized bulk of money, and two packages were small and full of different colored diamonds of all sizes. Along with the packages was a manilla envelope that was saran wrapped and put inside a Ziploc bag.

Joveezy grabbed the envelope and took it out of the Ziploc bag and began unraveling it. As he was doing that, he looked up at Banks and Rawdy and told them to get duffle bags to load up the packages and anything on the corpse they could keep.

When Banks and Rawdy left to go get the duffle bags, he opened the manilla envelope and looked inside. Inside was a note written on a ripped piece of paper along with some pictures. He pulled them out and looked at the pictures first. The pictures were of a bunch of Italians outside of a church and at a restaurant. In other pictures, the Italians were shaking hands with some Black men and a Black priest. After looking at the photo, he read the paper. It said, "Beware of the demon that lurks in the house of worship for they hide behind a mask of good, but underneath is the devil's puppeteers protecting what isn't theirs and they don't see." Below the note was a number He passed the note to Ced.

"This shit getting weirder and weirder, and I got the feeling we bout to get in deeper shit," Joveezy said to Ced.

Ced looked at Joveezy after reading the note and scanning through the photos. "Bro, what the fuck we *boing*, thug? What, we some type of extreme adventurists or some shit now? These photos are of some more Italian muthafuckers, and on top of that, they meeting up with some niggas who involved with a church of worship. But by this note the people at the church ain't right. And these numbers you looking at ain't just numbers. They coordinate with a location, Blood. I don't think we should get involved," Ced told Joveezy.

"Look, bro, what if these muthafuckas," he said, pointing to the pictures, "know something about why we being targeted and who setting us up? It's a road I'm willing to take. I mean, we already involved in deep pig shit anyway."

Ced shook his head, sighing. "Damn, bro, sometimes you gotta be smarter than the average scholar, my nigga. But fuck it. You know I'm riding with you to the end."

Banks and Rawdy came back and dropped down the duffle bags and climbed down to load the bags. as Joveezy and Ced climbed out. Once the bags were full and everything of value was removed from the casket, they took the shovels and headed back to the truck. They loaded into the truck and headed out of the cemetery, but before they could make it all the way out, two black Ford Raptor trucks blocked them at the exit.

"Fuck!" Joveezy exclaimed, immediately sensing danger, and put the G-Wagon in reverse. As he reversed the truck, the Ford Raptors turned into the cemetery and pursued.

"Who the fuck is these niggas? And how the fuck they know we would be here?" Ced questioned.

"Seems like somebody keeping tabs on us," Joveezy replied, as he put the truck in drive and turned down another road of the cemetery, looking for another way out. As he sped along, gunshots began to ring out from the Ford Raptor trucks. Rawdy and lil Loko rolled down their windows, hanging out far enough to return shots with their Glocks. As Joveezy sped along the cemetery road, another Ford Raptor truck was coming head on toward them. Joveezy took another road, just barely missing the turn. As he turned, the occupant of the truck that was in front of him began to shoot. The gunshots pinged off the side of Joveezy's truck.

"Oh, shit, they got brody. They got brody," Lil Loko yelled, pulling Rawdy's slumped body into the truck.

Hearing the commotion, Joveezy took a quick glance into the rear mirror to see what was going on. The whole right side of Rawdy's head was blown off. Parts of his exposed brains were falling out onto the seat of his G-Wagon. Joveezy looked ahead, eager and desperate to find an escape out of the cemetery and fast. To his luck, he found it and gunned the truck out into oncoming traffic, causing cars to blare their horns, swerve, and crash into other cars. One of the Ford Raptors that was following behind Joveezy rushed into traffic, slow to register what had just happened, and got caught up in the wreck, slowing down the other two Ford Raptors that were right behind it.

Joveezy seized the moment and quickly turned down a side street and found his way back onto the freeway, heading back to Ypsilanti. He looked over at Ced, who was quiet with his head leaning against the window on the passenger side. His face showed signs that he was hurt and in excruciating pain, and he was beathing shallowly. Joveezy looked closer and saw that Ced was holding his right side.

"Aye, bro, you good, homie? Talk to me!" Joveezy said with panic in his tone.

"Yeah, bro, it ain't shit. Just get me home," he said in a slow drawl. He coughed up blood before slumping forward and passing out.

"Fuuuck," Joveezy yelled.

Chapter 17

The incident at the cemetery in Detroit left Joveezy in a rage and wanting vengeance. Ced and Rawdy were rushed to the emergency room on the eastside of Detroit where Rawdy was announced dead, and Ced was rushed into surgery. Once Joveezy saw that Ced was in good hands, he immediately left to avoid any police questioning. He knew a couple of nurses he'd met a few years back who worked at the hospital that kept him updated on Ced's conditions. Ced underwent major surgery that included removing a ruptured kidney, putting pins in his hips, and giving him two blood transfusion. The bullet had passed through, so they didn't have to remove it. Other than that, doctors said he was stable and would be able to leave in a couple of weeks. Police would want a statement though, the nurse told Joveezy.

Rawdy's body would be released to his family after an autopsy report was done. Joveezy made sure to send his family one hundred thousand dollars and paid extra for the funeral services. He was furious that once again, someone was keeping a close eye on him and knew he would be at the cemetery. Shit was too surreal and getting out of hand. He placed some calls to Mike from a burner phone he bought and told him to set up an emergency meeting, giving Mike the location of where it would be held out in Taylor, Michigan. He needed to get to who was after him now besides the Feds, and he needed to get to the bottom of it asap.

After leaving the hospital and calling Mike, he went back to Ypsilanti to his home in West Willow and grabbed his money out of the safe, a couple of pistols, some clothes, and his French mastiffs, Tango and Bonnie, then placed a call to his personal mechanic who did all the detailing and custom work on his vehicles to have his G-Wagon fixed and restored. He put the shit from the cemetery up in the safe, called an Uber, and got a room at the Red Roof Inn for a few days in Taylor, Michigan that he had his Aunt Anita pay for in her name and paid her for doing it. He felt laying low was a must. Once he got settled in the Red Roof Inn, he called Lisa from the burner phone.

"Hello, who is this?" she answered sleepily.

"Baby, it's me. Sorry I had to call you from a different number. But I didn't want to call you from my line," he said.

"What's up, Daddy? You alright? I haven't heard from you in two whole days and been blowing you up. I thought you was coming back. What happened?"

Joveezy sighed before answering her questions. "Love, a lot happened, but I don't want to talk on the phone. We need to meet up somewhere, and I will explain everything to you."

"Okay, Daddy. You scaring me, babe. What do you mean some…"

"Look, Lisa," Joveezy said, cutting her off. "I told you I will explain shit to you when we meet up."

"Okay. Okay, Daddy. Where you want me to meet you at?"

"Meet me at the go-kart track in Taylor, Michigan tomorrow at 12 p.m., and baby, make sure you watch your back and not being followed."

"Okay, do you need me to do anything before I meet you out there?"

"No, sweetheart. I will see you tomorrow."

"Okay, I love youuuu and be safe, my king."

"Love you too, gorgeous," Joveezy replied before ending the call.

He got up, headed to the bathroom, and cut the shower on, letting it run for a few minutes to get hot. He undressed and took a long shower, while his mind drifted off, recounting his childhood. He could remember growing up in the rough parts of Detroit's eastside. Majority of the houses were run down in certain neighborhoods. There were a lot of vacant lots and fields, and the grass was unkept as well.

***

The crime and drug rate in Detroit was at an all-time high and had been for a long time. Josiah was eleven years old when he was staying on the eastside seven mile and Palmer Street and had been living in that neighborhood since the day he came from Grace Hospital. His mother and father were raising him with his four-year-old sister, Tracey, his two brothers, nine-year-old Quincy and thirteen-year-old Justice. Things weren't at all good at home. In fact, his mom never worked and was a heavy drinker, and although his pops worked at a grocery store loading groceries into bags and cleaning up aisles, it was hard to keep up with putting food on the table, let alone paying the bills on time, which led to a lot of fights between his mom and dad.

Josiah and his siblings barely went to school, so his teachers, knowing their situation, made sure to come by the house and drop off schoolwork. After his work was finished, he would slip out of the house and roam the streets rather than stay home. He would meet up with a couple of his friends, Santino and Jacarie, from school and get into mischief, stealing bikes from neighborhoods and breaking into abandoned houses.

In 2015, when he was thirteen, they decided to steal cars for the joyride. One day, Jacarie introduced one of his cousins to Josiah, an older teen of sixteen who stole cars too. He told them that they could make money stealing cars and take them to a chop shop that he knew would pay them fifteen hundred or more depending on what type of vehicle it was.

Josiah was intrigued at the mention of making money and was eager for the opportunity, so he, Jacarie, and Santino put together a crew of six, and they stole any car they could get into or was left idling at a gas station. The money they made off the cars was divided amongst each other, and Josiah bought him and his siblings' new clothes and shoes. His brothers never asked him how he got the money, just happy to be in fresh gear. Plus, their mom never paid too much attention to what he or the others were doing, let alone what was going on, because of her daily drinking binge. And their dad ended up pulling a second job at nights as a security guard at a strip club. By now, Josiah had been stealing cars for about three months. Two months before Josiah's fourteenth birthday, he decided to steal a car without his crew and stole a Corvette Z06, and before he could get out of the neighborhood, police surrounded the car, and he was arrested and sent to Juvenile for grand theft auto. Since it was his first offense, he ended up only getting a couple of months in Juvenile where he met Mohammed.

Mohammed was sixteen and had a laidback personality. He was well respected by a lot of the kids in the pod, and staff let him practically do whatever he wanted. He'd noticed Josiah's quietness for the past five days and how he kept to himself and approached him.

"Yo, man, what's up, homie? My name Mohammed," he said, extending his hand out to Josiah for a handshake.

Josiah look at his hand then up at him before shaking his hand. "My name is Josiah," he replied.

"Not to be invasive or nothing, but what you doing in here? You don't seem like the type of kid to be in no trouble. No disrespect."

Josiah looked down at his feet. "I got in trouble for stealing a car."

"Dang, man, how long they give you?"

"I got two months since it was my first offense."

"Man, they could have gave you just probation on your first offense. They played you, bro. How old are you?" asked Mohammad.

"Thirteen."

"Damn, you three years younger than me. What you out there stealing cars for?"

"Well, it was for fun, then somebody said I could make money, so I did. Just this time, I got caught."

"How much money you make stealing cars?"

Josiah hesitated for a moment before answering. "A bunch."

Mohammed laughed. "Okay, okay, I see you. I see you. You about hat money."

"Yeah," Josiah said. "I had to look out for me and my brothers and sister. What about you?"

"Got caught at the Diamonds Liquor Store on Six Mile and Conant selling rocks. When they pulled up, I took off running, threw the dope and pistol I had."

Josiah and Mohammed talked for about an hour, and from that day forward, they became good friends. During Josiah's last week and a half in Juvenile, Mohammed told him to reach out to his Uncle Reggie who could put him on if he wanted to make some quick and easy money instead of stealing cars. Josiah took him up on the offer and said he would reach out as soon as he was released. While they were talking, two female staff members came into the pod and told Josiah that his case worker needed to see him concerning a family emergency. A confused Josiah looked at Mohammed then got up and followed the staff out the pod. He was led to his case worker's office. Once inside, the two officers steeped out and closed the door, leaving Josiah and his case worker by themselves.

Ms. Vaughn was a tall, mocha colored woman. She was beautiful, in her early thirties, had hazel eyes, and her hair sat in curls on her shoulders.

"How are you doing today, Josiah?" she asked in a soft tone.

"Um, I'm okay, I guess."

"Are you sure? Do you need anything? Are you being treated right?"

"Yes, I am being treated right, and I want to go home."

Ms. Vaughn set back and studied Josiah with a sad look on her face. "Josiah, honey, I am so sorry to have to tell you this, sweetie, but something tragic has happened to your family. They were invoiced in a very bad car accident."

"Wha-what do you m-mean car a-accident?" Josiah asked with a tremble in his voice. "Who all w-was in the accident?"

Ms. Vaughn sighed. "Your mom, dad, your sister, and both of your brothers. Your mom was the driver and swerved into oncoming traffic and was hit by a semi which rolled the car eight times before catching fire and exploding seconds later. I'm so sorry, Josiah."

"When did this happen?" Josiah asked with tears in his eyes.

"This happened yesterday. Your Aunt Anita called to inform us of the incident, and we were told to let you know of the situation. And due to this incident, I took the liberty of calling your judge and getting you an early release. Since your aunt is next of kin and your mom's sister, the court has granted her custody of you for emergency purposes. You are set to be released tomorrow, okay?"

Josiah nodded his head, as the tears began to flow in rivers now.

Ms. Vaughn got up from her desk and hugged Josiah. "Stay out of trouble, okay? And when you get back to the pod, make sure you pack your things. You will be released early in the morning. And if you need anything, here's my number." She then opened the door and motioned for the two guards to take him back to the pod.

When Josiah got back to the unit, he ran up to his cell, closed the door, and cried into his pillow. Mohammed came to his cell to check up on him, and Josiah told him about his family and his early release. They chilled for a couple hours, and Josiah packed up his things and got ready for his release.

Joveezy cut the shower off and went to the bed area and got dressed. He wore a light outfit, a black V-neck t-shirt, black jeans, and black Forces. He grabbed Bonnie and Tango's leashes, put the leases on the dogs, and put a Glock 10 with a silencer on his hip. He headed out the door to his rental, put the dogs in the back of the car, got in the driver's seat, and jumped on the freeway, heading to Grand Rapids, Michigan.

Chapter 18

Joveezy cruised the suburban neighborhood in Grand Rapids in a grey, 2016 Audi Q3 2.0T Quattro Tiptronic rental. Tango and Bonnie were in the back, laying on the floor with their muzzles resting on their paws. But both were fully awake and on high alert with anticipation.

The suburbs was quiet at three-forty in the morning. No cars were about except the one he was driving, and not a soul stirred in the houses that had porch lights and streetlights that illuminated them.

After a few turns and twists through the suburban neighborhoods, the GPS navigation system in the truck notified Joveezy that he had arrived at his destination. Instead of stopping, he continued to cruise past the house while scoping out his surroundings and the layout, description, and details about the house, checking for any cameras as well. Once farther up the street, Joveezy parked his rental on the end of the street in front of a light blue and white house and cut off the Audi before exiting the vehicle. He grabbed a pair of black latex gloves and a black half mask that covered the nose and mouth of his face, put them on, and retrieved his Glock 10 with the silencer out of the glove compartment, checked to make sure a bullet was in the chamber, and put the gun on his hip. After that, he went to the back passenger door, opened it up, and grabbed Tango and Bonnie's leashes, while they both hopped out the vehicle and sniffed at the air. Joveezy closed the door softly but didn't lock the vehicle. He turned and headed back to the house the GPS led him to.

The house was a large, white house with a small front yard and a two-car garage connected to the house. A picture window decorated with pale yellow curtains overlooked the front yard. In the driveway sat a white Rubicon Jeep. A side path that led to the backyard was what Joveezy chose to take. A privacy fence stood at the back entrance, but it was not locked and stood open partly. Before Joveezy went in, he took the leashes off the French mastiffs, Tango and Bonnie, and put the leashes around his waist like a belt. Both Bonnie and Tango stood by his side and didn't move unless he did, but now that their leashes were off, their stance changed, ears pricked up, and they moved in a slow stealth like mode with all their senses on high alert.

Joveezy opened the privacy fence slowly so that the fence didn't creak on its hinges and make any noise. Once the fence was open to where he could walk through, he signaled for the French mastiffs to go before him. They entered the backyard at a slow pace, eyes on any movement or any detection of danger. Joveezy stayed close by them at a crouch, while they came farther into the backyard. Joveezy stopped, and when he stopped, so did the French mastiffs. He looked around the backyard and gave thanks to the fact that the occupants of the house didn't have any dogs out back nor did he see a doghouse. What did lay out in the backyard was a trampoline, an outside pool built into the ground with a jacuzzi, and a pavilion with a bench under it and a large grill. The grass smelled as if it had been recently cut, and the privacy fence that ran along the whole backyard was lined with roses and tulips.

After scoping out the backyard, he made his way to the back door of the house which were sliding doors. The sliding doors were connected to the dining room area of the house and gave him a clear view of what lay about inside, and if anyone was there, he would be able to tell. Satisfied, he checked the slider doors to see if they were unlocked, and to his surprise, they were unlocked. He shook his head, thinking, *Why would somebody just leave their doors unlocked in a neighborhood like this?* He slid the door sliders slightly and very quietly. Once it was opened, he pointed at Tango and Bonnie outside the sliders, and they both sat down and didn't move, even after he disappeared through the dining room and left he slider doors open. Joveezy pulled out his Glock 10 and began to make his way through the dining room. There were two entryways. One was right ahead of him, leading to the living room, and the entrance to his left led to the kitchen. He went straight ahead to the living room.

The living room was huge, and photos lined the walls along with certificates and a photo of a man shaking hands with the president, Trump. Other family photos lined the walls as well and newspaper clippings. Also on the wall was a ninety-inch flat screen television above a fireplace. Above the fireplace but below the TV were trophies and awards ranging from sports such as bowling, mixed martial arts, a gold medal for swimming, Purple Heart medal in a case, and a trophy in music for piano. The living room had a white leather couch in the shape of a "L" that had enough room to seat at least ten people. The couch looked like one of those movie theater couches. In the far corner of the living room sat a medium sized baby grand piano. Joveezy left out of the living room and walked into a hall. To his left were two doors next to each other.

He made his way to the two doors. The first door was the bathroom, and the second door was open just a crack for him to peek into. When he peeked into the room, he could make out a bookshelf along the wall from a small source of light that illuminate it from somewhere in the room and part of a desk.

He opened the door up a bit with his gloved hand, pistol at the ready, and entered the room in a crouch. No one was in the room; it turned out to be an office which had degrees and certificates on the walls and a picture of a man in military uniform. In another photo, he was in a suit and tie. On the desk sat a laptop computer, a small lamp that was left on, and stacks of files and folders. The desk had drawers attached that he opened. Inside the first drawer was some passports, a manilla envelope, a key, and a Luger 9 mm. He checked the contents of the manilla envelope and inside was some money. He put the manilla envelope back down and took the gun, popped the clip out, and checked to see if one was in the chamber before he put the clip behind some of the books on the shelf before he drew his focus back to the desk drawer.

After looking through the rest of the drawers, he scanned through the files on the desk and continued to look around the office. Next to the bookshelf was a tall, black cabinet that was closed. He tried to open it up, but it was locked. Remembering the key in the desk drawer, he returned to it and used the key to open the cabinet. The cabinet opened, and inside sat a military uniform, a couple of Teflon bulletproof vests, a MP-4, an AR-50, and some files on the top shelf. Joveezy picked up the files on the top shelf and looked through them. The files contained reports, photos of him, his crew, and some written reports. A second file contained more photos of Lacey, some Black priest, Nightmare, and some more Italians that Joveezy didn't recognized from previous photos or the warehouse. He immediately tucked the files on his waist and closed the cabinet, locked back up, and put the key back in the drawer. He then left the office, closed the door how he found it, and made his way back up the hallway. Before he went back to the living room, he noticed the front door and a set of stairs next to it.

Taking a mental note, he went back into the living room and dining room to the slider where Tango and Bonnie were waiting patiently. Joveezy made a soft clicking sound with his tongue, and both French mastiffs entered the house. He turned back around and made his way back to the stairs with Tango and Bonnie right by his side. As he made his way to the living room, Joveezy heard a set of footsteps overhead, and he froze in his tracks. Tango and Bonnie did too. Joveezy listened to the motion of the footsteps and followed it. The footsteps stopped somewhere above, and a few minute later, a toilet flushed. The footsteps could be heard again, and they sounded like they were moving in a different direction other than back the way they came from. He then heard footsteps coming down the stairs. With his pistol in his hand, he and the French mastiffs made their way back into the dining room, and Joveezy stood against the wall leading to the kitchen with Tango and Bonnie on the opposite side of him.

The footsteps made their way down the hallway into the kitchen, and seconds later, a microwave cut on. Joveezy ducked low and peeked around the corner into the kitchen. In the kitchen, on the other side of the kitchen island, was a man with his back turned to him at the microwave above the stove. He made his way to the man, came around the side of the counter, and popped up with the gun pointed at the man.

"Well, well, well. Look what we have here," Joveezy said. "Just like old acquaintances, we meet again, Agent Vincent."

Startled, Agent Vincent turned toward Joveezy and looked at him with wide eyes and fear in them. "Who are you, and w-what are you doing in my house?"

"Ain.t it funny how you forget about the people you harass until they right in your domain and don't have any clue as to who they are because you got a shit load of cases and a hundred or so different people you encounter? Now look at you," Joveezy stated.

"Look, man, what do you want? Money? I got plenty, man," Agent Vincent said.

"Oh, in due time you gonna find out what I want, and it ain't money. In the meantime, let's take a trip to your office."

"I'm not goin' anywhere…"

"Oh, you going where I say you going. Now, let's move, and I'm not going to say it again," Joveezy said, cutting Agent Vincent off with a hint of irritation n his voice.

Motioning with his gun, Joveezy stepped back and waved the gun back-and-forth, letting Agent Vincent know to move. Agent Vincent moved toward the office, watching Joveezy out the side of his eye. "Don't try any heroic shit either," Joveezy warned Agent Vincent, watching his body language and smiling to himself.

"No need to be nervous," he told him. "They just extra security and a pair of trustworthy eyes."

With his right leg, Joveezy tapped Bonnie lightly on her body, and immediately, she moved low to the ground as if stalking her prey. With her tail still and showing her teeth in a snarl, she moved closer to Agent Vincent, close enough to nip at him and get him to move at a quick but steady pace into the office.

Once they were inside the office, Joveezy closed the door and locked it. Agent Vincent was standing behind the desk. Bonnie and Tango were on opposite sides of the desk, watching Agent Vincent closely and eager to attack at the slightest hint of a threat.

"Sit down," Joveezy told Agent Vincent.

Agent Vincent sat down in the chair at his desk. "Look, man, what is it that you want?" he asked.

"I need you to answer some questions about an investigation you're actively working on at the time. And I ain't tryna hear about you can't answer any question because you will answer them if you and your family want to live."

"You leave my family out of this," Agent Vincent said, slightly raising his voice, face turning red.

Tango and Bonnie growled at the sudden aggression in Agent Vincent's voice, and he immediately checked his anger.

"As I was saying, Agent Vincent, you will give me the information I want if you and your family want to live, and before you try to lie to me, I got the files and statements on the investigation you're looking into," Joveezy said, pulling the files from the waistband of his pants and showing him the contents. "First, I want to know why and what you want to look into these particular people for. Oh, and before I forget to add, your investigation into this case was done illegally, so what's your agenda?"

Agent Vincent started to sweat with perspiration on his forehead and tugged at the collar of his t-shirt. "How did you get those files?" he asked, looking at the files on his desk.

"I ask the questions, not you. So, answer my questions, and I'm not going to keep repeating myself."

"Okay, okay, where do you want me to start?"

"Well, let's start with what led you to this investigation."

"It started a couple years ago when an anonymous caller claiming to have information about a big drug ring involving some Italians and a female named Lacey Cortez. The caller was so sure about her sources."

"Wait, so the caller was female?" Joveezy asked with raised eyebrows, showing confusion.

"Yeah, she said that she could give us the locations of drop off points where transactions would take place. The caller didn't give her name, but she promised to give more resources and people that would be of interest to us. I asked her her motives and why she was doing it, and she said she wanted to help us clean the streets up. When asked if she was seeking a reward or protection, she said no. Although it was a little strange, it sparked our interest, so we put a team together and did a ghost investigation on the information given to us before we decided if it was legit enough to open up a real investigation. It took us a few weeks of staking out our targets, and we were just about to give up our investigation until Lacey led us straight to the Italians at a restaurant and then a warehouse where, at both locations, duffle bags were exchanged between both suspects. In which, we took photos of each transaction. That got the ball rolling, and we decided to delve deeper into Lacey and the Italians, and one thing led to the next. After further investigation into the warehouse, we found out that it was abandoned but secretly used to run shipments of crates and drug smuggling. We recognized some of the Italians that were there who is on our FBI wanted list for being involved in a drug ring, homicide, kidnapping and disappearances of local police officers, and gun smuggling. So, it was determined that some type of drug operation was going on. Without information, we was allowed to keep up the investigation, and we continued to work with the anonymous caller as well. We eventually found out about the abduction of Lacey and her sudden reappearance back on the scene and how she blew up, dominating the underworld, so we started looking into the people she was involved with from friends to family members, and what we found out got spicier. Who interested us the most though was Josiah Johnson aka Joveezy. Looking further into him, we found out about the money he had and the companies he owned. Although we still couldn't figure out how he came into all that money, we decided to continue an investigation into Josiah and the people he associated with too and found out that he ran a crew. Although he moved under the radar and covered his tracks, the handful of people he ran with had an outstanding rap sheet. Although his account and business came back legit due to his girlfriend, Josiah eventually slipped up though like they all do and met a connect on a party yacht on a vacation trip he took two and a half years ago in Barbados. Ironic that the connect was a Mexican cartel drug kingpin who is also an informant for the FBI. Chino distributes over about one hundred thousand kilos of cocaine for us, covering from parts of the south to the Midwest and West Coast, and we catch our suspects because of him. In return, he stays out of jail. When Chino got back to the U.S., we paid him a visit and confirmed that Josiah and him arranged to do business.

He said Josiah requested twenty kilos, and if he liked the product, he would buy one hundred more.

"Here's the twist though. Josiah never personally made the orders himself. One of his close associates named Beno did. And he the one made the pickup. For two years, we investigated, and just when we thought we could come close to closing the case and make some arrests, something new comes up. Just recently, someone hit the Italians and left a wake of bodies. Whoever did it timed it perfectly because at that time, we didn't have that warehouse under surveillance. Our team had just packed it up for that night an hour and thirty-six minutes before the hit took place. We don't know who did it, but we think it's all connected. Word going around is that one of Josiah's people were bragging about a big lick they hit, and we suspect him to be talking about the warehouse in Detroit. If we can find out who he is, FBI is going to bring him in for questioning and get him to flip for a deal. Another big break in the case led us back to Lacey. Someone just tried to take her life and killed her boyfriend and his men. Local police interviewed her and let her go. Right now, we don't know where she's laying low. We told the local department to hold her for questioning, but they failed, so now, they're being held accountable for interfering with an ongoing FBI investigation and allowing a potential suspect to go free. The individuals that tried to kill Lacey were Colombian citizens here illegally and hired professional hitmen who are a part of the militia for the Colombian government. Whoever wanted Lacey dead meant to make sure she was taken care of swiftly, but for some reason, she got lucky enough to escape death. This is the biggest case we've had by far and deeper than what we expected. So many are involved that we have yet to reveal," Agent Vincent explained before finally taking time to catch his breath.

"So, how close are you to finishing the case now?" Joveezy asked.

"Not even close. Too many holes in the case."

"Is that all the info you got for me?"

"Yeah, as best as I could tell you and to the point."

"You sure you not holding nothing from me?"

"Yeah, man, I'm sure."

Joveezy reached up to his face and took the half mask off his face, and when it came off, the agent looked at Joveezy in disbelief and pure hatred. "You son of a bitch, how did you find me? And the balls you have!"

"That doesn't matter now, do it, Vincent? What matters is we here now, and I appreciate you for the information you shared with me," Joveezy said before pulling the trigger, hitting Agent Vincent between the eyes. The silencer barely made a sound. Vincent's body slumped forward onto the files on his desk.

He put his half mask back on, as he and the French mastiffs exited the office. He went to the kitchen, went to the stove, and examined it. The stove was a gas stove, an older model for such a nice house. He looked at the time on the stove and then at his watch. It was four thirty-eight a.m. He went behind the stove and unplugged the gas tube connected to the stove and turned the value up on the gas until it hissed out of the hose.

He then searched the kitchen drawers until he found some candles. He retrieved four medium sized candles and went into the living room and lit them before he set them above the fireplace where the awards and trophies sat.

With the French mastiff at his heels, he left back out through the dining room and back through the slider doors. He locked the sliders from the inside and closed them quietly. He took the leashes from around his waist and latched them back onto the collars of both Tango and Bonnie. He then headed out the fence of the backyard, closed it, and headed back to his truck and left the suburban neighborhood.

Outside of the suburban neighborhood was a gas station, and across from there was a small shopping center. He drove in the shopping center and parked there with his window rolled down a crack. By now, it was five twenty a.m.

Some of the stores were already opening or just now opening up. After about ten minutes, he heard what he had been listening for. The explosion was louder than he thought, and it rocked the suburban neighborhood to the point he thought he felt a small tremble. Satisfied, he left the area and headed back to the freeway and to the meeting location he had set up with Mike and his crew and Lisa.

Chapter 19

The Detroit news was raving about the endless occurrence of violence soaring throughout the city. Fox 2 News had great ratings with the murder rate being at its highest in over twenty years. One of the main headlines that had been buzzing at the center of attention was the farmhouse massacre that took place in southwest Detroit that resulted in the death of at least twenty or so armed men.

"An anonymous call was made to local police reporting gun shots being heard that the caller said lasted for at least fifteen minutes or more. Sources cannot yet identify the motive or what led to this deadly shootout, but the FBI has taken over the investigation and is now handling the case. Sources also say that before the FBI arrived, another shootout took place between local police and unknown suspects, leaving eight police officers dead and three dead suspects before the other unknown suspects fled the scene. At this time, we have no further information about the events that took place here, but we do know that this is an ongoing investigation. And the FBI is keeping this situation tightly under wraps.

"Also, there are reports coming in just recently that there has been reports made of a high-speed shootout on the eastside of Detroit at the Greenwood Cemetery, leading to a pile up. Sources also report that there was a shootout between the police who arrived on the scene and armed suspects, leaving two officers dead, one critically injured, and one suspect dead before the other suspects fled the scene in two black Ford Raptor trucks and taking a third vehicle at gun point. There were no other casualties reported, but in both cases, suspects were wearing camouflage gear and body armor. There is a statewide search for the suspects, as they have yet to be identified. But if you see these trucks, please do not try to be a hero and immediately call the police, as these suspects are armed and very dangerous. This has been your spokesperson, Amanda Parnell, with the Fox 2 News."

Keara cut the TV off and turned to Lacey and Dee-Dee. Tonya and Angelica had arrived a couple hours after Lacey to be by her side and comfort her while she grieved.

"Damn, Lace, this shit is deeper than the trenches, girl. What we gone do?" asked Keara.

Lacey looked in the distance with anger and frustration in her eyes, lost in thought, before answering. "I'm going to find Dominic and that bitch, Madame Charity, and kill them. I still cannot believe they found me and killed Nightmare and his whole security. It doesn't make sense how they knew where we were. It just doesn't. It's like everywhere I go, a pair of eyes are there watching my every move."

"Someone most definitely keeping tabs on you," Angelica said, "but who is the question. And could they be watching us now?"

"I hope not," Keara said before peeking out the window.

"Look, right now, we need to focus on who the snake is. Could it be one of Nightmare's own men? I never did trust majority of them and neither did you, Lacey," Dee-Dee pointed out.

"Yeah, but I don't think Nightmare's men would betray him or do some shit like that though," Lacey responded.

"For the right price and better opportunity, they would. Niggas are grimy like that, Lace," Tonya chimed in with a distant look on her face, "and you should know that. What if one of his men did cross you and Nightmare over? The question still remains *why*?"

"Look, don't nothing make sense," Keara said. "I think we just need to figure out the obvious – who missing out the dead and unaccounted for of Nightmare's men, where he hiding out, and we unmask the punk bitch like that. If he got contact with Dominic or that bitch, they may know they location as well."

"Yeah, it seems like a shot we can take," Dee-Dee agreed. "I can hit up some of my contacts at the city morgue and get a list of all the bodies that came through, and we can determine who unaccounted for. Some of Nightmare's men were there the night Lacey and Dominic had that meeting, and shit hit the fan. Nightmare didn't like the idea of us being setup and led into a trap, which it turned out to be."

"Okay, so my question is are you going to hold a funeral for Nightmare and his cousin or have him cremated?" Keara asked.

"Bitch, is you serious right now?" Angelica asked, looking at Keara with a sideways glance. "Do you think she want to hold a funeral and set herself…"

"Actually," Lacey said, cutting Angelica off, "I do want to go through with holding his funeral. I already made a decision to have his wake and funeral in the next four days, and I am advertising it in the newspapers and paying the news to announce it on TV but not stick around to attend."

Everyone looked at her with a confused look on their faces except Dee-Dee.

"Okay, do you think that will be the best idea, Lace? Parading yourself out there in the open after what just happened? I mean, that's baiting yourself, sis," Keara expressed.

"That's the point – to draw out the wolves if they thirsty enough for blood, and obviously, these muthafuckas are and don't care about shit, not even the police, as you seen on the news. I figure, hold the funeral and see who gone pop up. Plus, I'm a woman, so people expect me to still throw a funeral because me and Nightmare were together.

"The plan is to have as much security as possible out there. I still got a few hittas from out in Cali and other places that will be out here later today, plus my Arab connect still owe me favors. Oh, and Uncle Don got some niggas who ex-military and at my beck and call," Lacey said.

"Yeah, and I made sure to pick out a plot where we can see who coming in and out and avoid any unexpected surprises," Dee-Dee added.

"But what about the kids and families that might show up? And are we forgetting that the FBI involved in this shit now? What if they decide to show up and be nosey?" asked Angelica.

"No kids or families gone be there because Nightmare don't have any family left that he fuck with. His only family getting buried with him. His mom died from cancer when he was eight, and his dad died in Iraq when Nightmare was still a baby. His only other relatives is his cousin, Menace, and his mom took Nightmare in when his mom died. Menace's mom died three years ago from a stroke, and it's been just Nightmare and Menage, and them two niggas been inseparable since they were kids. Besides that, Nightmare only had connects he dealt with and very few people he handled business with, and as far as FBI, I don't think they gone show up. They probably think it was a hit on Nightmare and not me."

"Do you think your plan will work?" asked Tonya.

"It's a long shot, but I have to," Lacey answered. "Look, y'all, my mind just fucked up right now, and I'm tired."

"Well, girl, you need to rest up and be at your best, babe. This is a stressful and tiring career and line of work," Angelica replied. "You pulled through worser shit though."

"Yeah, plus we need you to get back in focus for this funeral," said Tonya. "Also, are you going to the farmhouse?"

"No," Lacey said. "For one, if I got found there once already, who's to say they won't come back looking? Plus, the Feds got too much illegal shit out there. I don't want to get questioned. All I had there were clothes and shit like that, nothing serious or that can't be replaced."

"The Feds gone come for you eventually and get to questioning you," predicted Tonya, "especially when you hold his funeral."

"Yeah, I know, but until then, I will avoid them until that time comes."

Everyone was quiet for a while until Keara broke the silence. "So, what we do in the meantime?"

"In the meantime, we prepare for the funeral and then gather our resources and prepare for blood and mayhem," answered Dee-Dee.

"Alright, I will let my man, Sevyn, know I need him and his boys. They will do whatever I tell him. Plus, I got other niggas who small timers that move shit for me and can get information," Keara revealed.

"You really trust that nigga, Sevyn?" Lacey asked.

"Yeah."

"Alright, setup a meeting with me and him after the funeral. I got a proposition for him. If you really trust him, I'ma put him and his niggas in a position that can help them out a lot."

"I'll let him know," Keara said.

"Are you sure you want to go that route?" Dee-Dee asked Lacey. "We don't know if we can trust him or if he got ties that could lead back to Dominic and risk being betrayed again."

"Yeah, well, we gon' find out. And I'ma make him a special offer. It seems like Dominic and Madame got a army behind them that's impenetrable, and I need to get through the heart of it. Besides, ain't no telling who they got stalking me. Better safe than sorry."

"Alright, Lacey. If you content, then so am I," stated Dee-Dee.

"Me too," agreed Tonya.

"Me third," Angelica affirmed.

"You already know I'm in it till the end, cousin," Keara said.

"Oh, yeah, before I forget," Lacey said, "I need to get ahold of someone who would kill everyone in the world for me, and I would do the same for him. That's been like my twin since we were kids."

"Who you talking about?" Keara asked, puzzled.

"She talking about a nigga who's real dangerous and swift as a phantom when he wants to be incognito, and you know who he is, bitch. Quit playing dumb," Dee-Dee said to Keara.

"You talking about…"

"Josiah," Lacey finished for Angelica. "It's time that I get in touch with him. He the reason Nightmare found me anyway. Nightmare heard I was missing, and he reached out to him. Once they rescued me, Josiah stuck around long enough to make sure I was good and went back to doing his thing."

"Bitch, that nigga is so fine, and his bitch yummy. I want him and her so bad," Angelica admitted with a daydreamy look in her eyes and a huge grin on her face.

"Oh, my God," expressed Keara, shaking her head at Angelica before turning her attention back to Lacey. "Shit really bout to hit the fan now, especially if you reaching out to cousin."

"Yup, and now, the games about to shift. Plus, it's been awhile. Josiah knows me better than anyone, and right now, he gone be my strength and means to end this shit. And this the best time to summon the phantom to flesh. After the funeral and once we figure out what we need, I'ma hit him up. In the meantime, we lay low and gather info."

Chapter 20

It was 10:20 a.m. when Joveezy arrived at the go-kart track back in Taylor. Although it was early, there was still a lot of people starting to show up. Saturday mornings at the go-kart track was always the busiest. Beside go-karts, they had batting cages, mini golf, concession stands, arcade games, and other fun activities.

The sun was rising high in the sky and had started to boom. Joveezy popped the hatch of the Audi and allowed Tango and Bonnie to rest in the back of the Audi rather than sit in the back on the floor. Although he left the hatch open, he still left the A.C. on in the vehicle.

Joveezy sat in the back with the French mastiffs and waited for Mike and everyone else to arrive. Around 10:45, Mike showed up in his grey Mercedes Benz S-Class. Soon after, Beno showed up in a black BMW X3 M401, Mouse pulled up in a red Ford Mustang Shelby GT500 Special Edition, and Nico, Craig, and Chris showed up in Nico's tan Mercedes Benz G-Class G-500.

Joveezy had picked a spot away from the activity to park so that there were available parking spaces for Mike, Beno, Mouse, and Nico to park next to him. Once they all showed up, they met Joveezy at the Audi. Tango and Bonnie stood up in the back of the Audi and growled at them. Joveezy soothed them, and they settled down.

"Damn. nigga, you got them big muthafuckas wit' you?" Beno asked.

"Yeah, I was staying out of Ypsi for a few days. So, I took them with me. Plus, I needed them for some shit," Joveezy said.

"So, how Ced doing?" asked Mike.

"He pulled through, but that nigga had to get two blood transfusion, a kidney removed, pins in his hips, and he gone be walking with a walking stick."

"Damn, Blood, dat shit fucked up," Nico expressed. "What the fuck happened?"

"We went to Detroit to check into some shit, and some niggas was there, waiting on us. The niggas was in three black Ford pick-ups like them sporty type trucks and was on our asses, shooting at us. Lil Loko and Rawdy was with us and started shooting back. Rawdy got half his head blown off, then I realized Ced was hit too. Lil homie, Rawdy, laying on a slab in the hospital morgue right now. I wired his people some money when I left the hospital yesterday. I took them niggas on a chase and ended up losing them in them trucks."

"Where was y'all at when they slid on y'all?" Mike asked.

"We was at the cemetery. I ended up coming across some shit at the warehouse demo that led me to check out some shit."

"What you find out?" asked Beno.

"A gravesite," Joveezy said. half telling everything. "It's crazy how shit happened though. It's like someone expected somebody to show up. We just happened to be that somebody who got caught up in the mix."

"Why a graveyard though? And what could possibly be there?" asked Mike.

"Maybe they wanted the niggas they were originally after to be closer to they resting place." Mouse chuckled. "Just fucked up y'all had to be there."

"Yeah, but I feel like all this shit is deeper than what we already know. And by Lacey being involved, she connected to this shit and the key to this. Plus, the Feds on her ass too, and now, they on us big time," Joveezy explained, pulling out the files he took from FBI Agent Vincent's house.

"Damn, where you get these?" asked Nico.

"I paid that bitch as federal agent who held me for questioning a visit."

"Man, I hope you slept dat bitch ass nigga," Beno exclaimed.

"Nigga, what the fuck you think I did, nigga? What you thought? I was just there to be there?" Joveezy stated with a little irritation in his voice.

"Naw, Blood, I ain't mean it like that, Slime," Beno assured.

"Then why the fuck would you say some stupid ass shit like that, nigga?" Joveezy questioned, hopping off the back of the Audi.

Beno took a few steps back. "Bro, I said I ain't mean it like that. Damn, Ru."

"Man, Beno, yo' ass tweaking, especially questioning big Slime. Yeah, you definitely tweaking," Craig chimed in. "Man, big bro, what we gone do about the other FBI agent, and do you got an idea who tried to get down on you and bro?"

"Well, for one, that other FBI agent, Dom, might be on high alert with extra security and harder to get to because of his partner's death, and if he suspect that his partner was murdered, Feds gonna be buzzing all over, and the news 'bout to be breaking news all day – if it ain't already. And I still don't know who tried to take us out. That's what I want to find out since this shit just happened last night."

"The news already talking about an FBI agent, Vincent, and his house exploding with him and his family in it. They said they don't know what caused it or if it was an accident or not, but FBI looking into it," Chris spoke for the first time since arriving.

"Well, that should buy us a little time to get to that other FBI agent and knock him out the way too," said Beno

"Yeah, but we gone eventually have to face the whole bureau once they find out who behind it," predicted Mouse.

"I mean, we gotta face them soon anyway," said Craig. "We already under Fed's radar, and once they got a hold of you, they don't 'let go, and I refuse to give my life to them bitches. I rather die."

"Aye, speaking of which, what did the FBI Agent Vincent expose to you about the case?" Mike asked Joveezy.

"All this shit started with an anonymous caller who put the Feds onto all of us, and whoever it is know Lacey and know about me and everybody. That's how the Feds got onto us and been watching us for a couple years. Also, we got a nigga in our family speaking on shit about the warehouse shit. Feds tryna figure out who he is, so they can get him to flip, and that bitch ass nigga, Chino, an FBI informant like we suspected, and he another reason Feds on our ass. That nigga been supplying niggas and setting them up to get busted for years. Why they ain't hit us yet or you, Beno, is still unknown. But I need you to get rid of the SRT8. That muthafucka hot, Blood."

"I got rid of it and sold it to a nigga down south the same day we had that last meeting," Beno said.

"About Chino," Chris began, "when we gon' slide on that rat ass bitch?"

"As a matter of fact, I want you, Beno, and Craig to put together a team of fifteen niggas. Slide on him in three weeks from now. Beno know where he posted up, so y'all can slide on him there. He gone have heavy security because he cartel, so I want y'all to do full surveillance and get the layout of his domain for the next couple of weeks. And when it's time to hit him, use all heavy artillery and explosives. Mike, you and Nico close down the spots asap. Use U-Hauls to move everything out of this bullshit and make sure they got security. Chris, you find out who speaking about that lick and take care of it and get some info about them black Fords. See if you luck up," Joveezy ordered them.

Mike and Nico immediately pulled out their phones and started making calls.

"I'm a take care of that other FBI agent. Until then, y'all know what need to be done," he said, ending the meeting.

After Mike and Nico finished up their calls, they told Joveezy that all spots from the Greens to the projects and the spot in Liberty Square were shut down, and five U-Haul trucks were being picked up now, and they all got into their cars and left. Joveezy sat back into the back of the Audi rental, lost in thought. He drifted to the events that had happened and were about to unfold. He thought about Lisa and most of all, Lacey. Lacey was his main focus. He needed to get in contact with her and let her know what he knew.

It was 11:50 a.m. when his burner phone rang. He answered. "Hello."

"Hey, Daddy. I'm pulling up in the go-kart place now. Where you at?" Lisa asked.

"Baby, I'm in the back. You will see me," he told her, stepping from the Audi, motioning to the French mastiffs to stay put. He went in the parking lot. "Do you see me? I'm by the gray Audi."

"Yes, Daddy, I see you," Lisa said and hung up.

Lisa pulled up in the grey on black Hellcat Charger and parked next to the Audi. She got out and ran to Joveezy and embraced him with a tight hug and kisses. She wore a green summer dress with gold hearts on the bottom trim of the dress. The dress came above her knees, and it hugged her body. She had her hair in a bun with a pair of Gucci glasses on her face and a fat, gold Cuban link around her neck. She wore no makeup except for light pink lipstick.

Joveezy squeezed her ass cheeks, while he kissed her passionately. They released from each other's embrace, and Lisa started to hit him with a barrage of questions.

"Daddy, what's going on? What happened? Why did you have to call me from a different number? Why haven't you called me? Where is the Trackhawk? Why you driving this car instead of the Trackhawk or the Mercedes truck? Are you okay? Did something happen at your house? Why we have to meet up all the way out here? Why don't you just move in with me? Or how bout we buy a house together? Are you in more trouble? Baby, please tell me what's going on. I been so worried about you. Scared something…"

"Lisa…"

"…ing happened to you. I don't know what would happen if I were to lose you, bae. I swear I would lose my mind and couldn't live without you, Da…"

"Lisa!" Joveezy raised his voice a little and gave her a shake on her shoulders to get her attention.

"Huh?" she asked, looking him in the eyes.

"Baby, slow down, sweetheart," he said, giving her a kiss on her soft, plush lips. "I'ma explain everything to you, okay? Just chill."

"Sorry, Daddy. I was just so worried about you, and these questions been eating at me. Sorry. I'm so sorry."

Joveezy began to tell Lisa everything he felt she should know about minus the robbery and the drugs and of course the killing of the FBI agent. He did tell her about the incident in Detroit at the cemetery last night and what happened to Ced and his lil homie, Rawdy.

"Oh, my God, bae," Lisa exclaimed with a shaky voice, as she put her hands to her mouth, tears now running down her cheeks.

"Baby, it gone be okay."

'She shook her head. "I knew something was wrong, bae. I felt it. That's why I always try to keep you home with me, but you always find a way to slip away from me. Baby. what if you got hurt? Then what? Where that leaves me?" Lisa sobbed.

"Baby, I'ma be alright. I promise you."

"I can't tell, the way you keep running into these strange occurrences lately. First, FBI and now, people shooting at you. Baby, what is going on?"

"I don't know, and that's what I need to figure out, love."

"Well, from what you told me, Lacey prat of this mayhem, so you need to reach out to her," she said, sniffling.

"I know, baby."

"Please get this stuff taken care of, bae. I need you more than anything, and I can't afford to lose you, especially not now."

"Baby, I'ma handle it."

"Okay, Daddy," Lisa said, wiping her tears. "Well, I want to tell you a couple things. Both are good news, or I hope at least it will brighten up our day for the moment."

"Oh, yeah. What is it?"

"We have a potential business proposal with the real estate company. This lady, Charity Victorian, made an offer that I couldn't pass up. She wanted to invest twenty-six million into the business toward buying condos and lake houses and houses worth at least a mil with this deal. She wants to own twenty-one percent of the business, and she would give us an extra five million every year to use at our own discretion. This deal is supposed to be finalized in the next three to four weeks. What do you think?"

"It sounds like a reasonable deal. Let's do it," Joveezy said. "Plus, she sounds like she got a lot of money to give away, especially if she giving us an extra five million a year on top of that twenty-six million. That's unheard of."

"I'm so excited, Daddy. We steady progressing with our businesses, and she owns an import/export enterprise that she is allowing us to invest in in Colombia. That's a big opportunity for us because now we can use cargo ships to transport and ship to and from overseas. That's another gateway to starting another business."

"Damn, for real?" Joveezy asked, now interested at the fact that he could own cargo ships. His mind started racing.

"Yup, we just need to find out what we gone transport and to where and from where. We have to get contracts for one and take orders and find out what's allowed and what's not allowed in the United Staes. Plus, we need to find out what port we gone use. I was thinking the Port of L.A."

"When did these deals take place?"

"I got a call from her lawyers this morning before I left to come meet you here. After a short and brief conversation, they faxed the contract to me and said that once that contract was looked over and signed, I could have it back. They faxed me an extra copy of the contract to have our lawyers look over, which I'ma do. Once the contract is finalized, then we get the money and a new investor," Lisa said excitedly.

"Okay, okay." Joveezy was excited for Lisa. "I'm so proud of you, baby. You handling your shit like a true queen."

"Thank you, Daddy."

"Now, what's this other news you wanted to tell me, love?"

Lisa straightened up and hesitated for a moment. "Baby, I'm uh…" She took a deep breath. "Um, Daddy? You uh… You about... You about to be a daddy," she let out, looking into Joveezy's eyes.

Joveezy looked back into her eyes, and he smiled a huge smile. "Baby, are you serious? You really pregnant?"

"Yes, Daddy, I'm pregnant," she said more comfortably and with laughter.

"Baby, you not pranking me, are you?" he asked with a serious face.

"Nope, Daddy. I took four pregnancy tests in the last three days, and it's legit. For the past two and a half weeks, I been having morning sickness, but I wasn't too sure. At first, I thought I was just getting sick, but it would always pass. When it kept happening, I knew the symptoms were what it was, and I missed my period, so I took the test, and all four tests say positive. I set up a doctor's appointment for Wednesday coming up."

"Fuck yeah, baby. We about to be parents. That is good news. Better yet, the best news so far," Joveezy said, hugging and kissing Lisa.

As Joveezy and Lisa held and kissed each other with excitement, a grey Cadillac truck cruised by them and exited the go-kart parking lot.

To Be Continued…

Turn the page for an early preview of the next installation to the *Blood and Mayhem* series.

Blood and Mayhem 2

Raul set in the driver's seat of a porcelain grey, bulletproof Cadillac truck, as he watched the events that took place at the go-kart track in Taylor, Michigan between Joveezy and his men and now him and his female friend who'd just arrived minutes prior. Instead of the trap at the cemetery being sprung by Lacey, who it was meant to be for originally, Joveezy got caught up in the triangle and became a part of it. After finding out that Joveezy was just as valuable as Lacey and that they were related, Madame Charity had a newfound interest and one that would bring her closer to having Lacey in her grasps once again. Once Madame Charity found out about Joveezy and the business he and his girlfriend owned, she took advantage of an opportunity and struck a deal with Lisa that was set to be finalized in the next few weeks.

"Madame, shall we continue to follow our target?" asked Raul, looking into the rearview mirror at the beautiful woman with jet-black hair, a high yellow skin tone, and dark, piercing eyes, as she sat in the back of the truck quietly. The look in her eyes brought unnerving chills down his spine.

"No, I have all that I need for now. There's no need to rush into things when you have everything at your feet already," said Madame Charity, staring out the window at her couple.

She then looked over at the person sitting next to her. "Seems like you were right, Dominic. Our friend here is as realistic as we know it and as deadly, especially after the little run in at the cemetery and then the trip he took to the house in Grand Rapids. It seems Joveezy and Lacey, out of sheer coincidence, got connections. She will force them to cross paths and very soon.

"Besides, blood is way thicker than water. And from what you tell me, Dominic, they have a close bond. How marvelous, but let's see if we can taint that bloodline."

Dominic looked over at Madame Charity. "Yes, Madame, it seems so, and I know we can get closer to Lacey now that we have her cousin. It was smart making that investment deal. He seems to be a successful individual but still dabbles in the streets. But the question is how close can we get to this to befriend him and gain his trust?"

"Getting to him isn't the issue." Madame Charity smiled to herself. "He loves and lusts for beauty and things. I can tell by how delicate and protective he is of those closest to him. And with him, it seems trust is a must. And if you have his trust, it seems loyalty will be never-ending. All he needs is another goddess by his side to help keep him focused. The closer I can get to him, the better. His girlfriend may be the key to his heart. If I can win her heart, I can win his. Besides, I cannot afford to let him slip through my fingers."

Dominic looked at Madame Charity. She was definitely a gorgeous woman, but to him, she seemed too big headed for her own good sometimes. But she was smart and knew what she was doing and what she wanted.

Charity Victorian's family was a very powerful family who lived in Colombia. They owned cocaine fields where they produced and extracted from the cocaine leaves and sold its treasures at the highest rate. Her father, his father, and his father's father were successful drug lords and over the years became more powerful and richer.

Charity Victorian was only six when she first came to realize how powerful her father was. One day while she was playing in the hallway of their mansion that overlooked the ocean, in the distance, on the second floor, she heard a commotion. Curious, she ventured to the patio connected to a bedroom overlooking the front yard of the mansion and peeked out between the guard railing bars on the patio to see two men dressed in green camouflage gear with AK-47 rifles over their shoulders. In between them was a man. Her father stood over the man and removed the hood. The man on his knees looked around, taking in the scenery. As he realized where he was at and who was in front of him, he became frantic and began pleading for mercy.

"N-No, please, brother. Y-you don't have to do this. I promise I will g-get it back. J-just give me some time, Julio," the man pleaded.

'Time? You had all the time you needed to steal from me, brother, your own flesh and blood, and you steal from my child when you steal from me. I gave you everything you wanted, and it still wasn't enough for you, Xavier. You are a disgrace to me and the Victorian family bloodline. This is why Papa never trusted you to take over the family business. You a snake, Xavier, and for that, you must answer to it," Julio Victorian said.

Julio reached one hand behind his back, and when he brought it back in front of him, he held a gold plated 1911 .45 with a red handle and shot Xavier Victorian point blank in his head. Blood and brain matter splattered on the two men's pants and the ground beside them. Julio waved to the men to get rid of the body and told them to have someone clean up the mess.

Chasity Victorian wasn't at all scared at what she saw happen before her eyes, instead curious and intrigued. Her father looked up at the patio and saw his daughter and smiled. Charity smiled back and waved at her father. When he waved back, she got up and went back inside the mansion and continued playing with her dolls.

Over the years, Charity began to shadow her father, listening and learning from him. He taught her the history of her family lineage and taught her that family should never betray each other. He put her in charge of handling the family accounts and business transactions at the age of thirteen. Her mother had died giving birth to her, so her father raised her with the help of maids and servants who were loyal to the family. She was the only child. And due to her father's illegal affairs and lifestyle, the rest of her family stayed away from her and her father except for a few, but her father made sure she would never go without.

The reign of her father in Colombia was a lasting but busy one. He was deep into politics and was an outstanding hierarchy and patriot in Colombia. Then, things changed suddenly when an ambitious Colombian family decided to try and take power for themselves by trying to overthrow her father and steal land, cocaine fields, and even setting fires to some of the field and killing some of Julio's armed men in the process, which started a war. A year after the war started, her father was killed in a car explosion that was rigged to a car bomb device, activated by a cell phone. Charity was only seventeen at that time, and no one else knew how to run the family business better than her because of the knowledge she gained over the years. And instead of grieving over her father's death, she took over the family business and gained more power in honor of her father. Soon, those who were loyal to her father became her loyal supporters, and she sought revenge on those who murdered her father.

After two years of war with the Octavio Colombian family, Charity finally put an end to them and took back full control of what belonged to her family. And with a newfound and deeper respect, she became known as Madame Charity Victorian, a young and powerful queen and heir to the Victorian family throne and a natural born war goddess.

"Raul, take me to the airport. I've seen and got what I want for now."

"Yes, Madame Charity," Raul said, putting the grey Cadillac truck into drive and cruising past Joveezy and Lisa and exiting the go-kart parking lot.

"Dominic, call my pilots and tell them to have the jet ready for takeoff. I shall be heading home to Colombia. I miss home and have important matters to attend to," she said.

Lock Down Publications and Ca$h Presents Assisted Publishing Packages

Due to an increase in the price of services we have increased our prices. The prices below reflect the price increase as of 11/1/24.

BASIC PACKAGE **$699** Editing Cover Design Formatting	**UPGRADED PACKAGE** **$1000** Typing Editing Cover Design Formatting Upload eBooks to Amazon Upload Paperback to Amazon
ADVANCE PACKAGE **$1,400** Typing Editing (line editing/content) Cover Design Formatting Copyright Registration Proofreading Upload eBooks to Amazon Upload Paperback to Amazon	**LDP SUPREME PACKAGE** **$1,700** Typing Editing (line editing/content) Cover Design Formatting Copyright Registration Proofreading Set up Amazon Account Upload eBooks to Amazon Upload Paperback to Amazon Advertise on LDP's Amazon and Facebook Page

***

Other services available upon request.
Additional charges may apply

Lock Down Publications
P.O. Box 944
Stockbridge, GA 30281-9998
Phone: 470 303-9761
Email: lockdownpublications@gmail.com

Submission Guideline

Submit the first three chapters of your completed manuscript to ldpsubmissions@gmail.com. In the subject line add **Your Book's Title**. The manuscript must be in a Word Doc file and sent as an attachment. Document should be in Times New Roman, double spaced, and in size 12 font. Also, provide your synopsis and full contact information. If sending multiple submissions, they must each be in a separate email.

Have a story but no way to send it electronically? You can still submit to LDP/Ca$h Presents. Send in the first three chapters, written or typed, of your completed manuscript to:

LDP: Submissions Dept
P.O. Box 944
Stockbridge, GA 30281-9998

DO NOT send original manuscript. Must be a duplicate. Provide your synopsis and a cover letter containing your full contact information.

Thanks for considering LDP and Ca$h Presents.

NEW RELEASES

BLOODLINE OF A SAVAGE 1-3
THESE VICIOUS STREETS 1-3
RELENTLESS GOON 1-3
BY PRINCE A. TAUHID

THE BUTTERFLY MAFIA 1-3
BY FUMIYA PAYNE

A THUG'S STREET PRINCESS 1&2
BY MEESHA

CITY OF SMOKE 3
BY MOLOTTI

GET IT IN SLUGS 1 &2
BY B. STALL

STANDING ON HER BUSINESS 1&2
BY DG SANTANA

STEPPERS 1,2&3
THE REAL BADDIES OF CHI-RAQ
BY KING RIO

THE LANE 1&2
BY KEN-KEN SPENCE

THUG OF SPADES 1&2
LOVE IN THE TRENCHES 2
CORNER BOYS
BY COREY ROBINSON

TIL DEATH 3
BY ARYANNA

THE BIRTH OF A GANGSTER 4
BY DELMONT PLAYER

PRODUCT OF THE STREETS 1-3
BY DEMOND "MONEY" ANDERSON

NO TIME FOR ERROR
BY KEESE

MONEY HUNGRY DEMONS 1-2
BY TRANAY ADAMS

HUB CITY MENACE 1-3
BY J. WHITE

A THUGGISH PASSION 1&2
LAND OF DA HOOLIGANZ 1-4
KILLAZ ON STANDBY 1&2
BY IRA B.

FO'EVA ROLLIN 1&2
BY ASSA RAYMOND BAKER

THE LEVEL UP 1&3
BY LUXURY KING

Coming Soon from Lock Down Publications/Ca$h Presents

IF YOU CROSS ME ONCE 6
ANGEL V
By Anthony Fields

A THUGS STREET PRINCESS 3
By Meesha

CORNER BOYS 2
By Corey Robinson

THA TAKEOVER
By Keith Chandler

BETRAYAL OF A G 2
By Ray Vinci

SAVAGE FAMILY EMPIRE 1&2
SOULLESS GOON 1,2&3
THE DIRTY SIDE OF MONEY 1,2&3
By Prince

FOR MY ENEMY'S SAKE
AMBITIONS OF A SLIDER
FRESH OFF DA PORCH
By IRA B.

BY THE TRUCKLOAD 1-4
TIPPIN' THE SCALES 1-3
BAD BITCHES WIT GUNZ 3
PROBLEM SOLVED 2
By Christopher "Diesel" Hornezes

Available Now

RESTRAINING ORDER 1 & 2
By **CA$H & Coffee**

LOVE KNOWS NO BOUNDARIES 1-3
By **Coffee**

RAISED AS A GOON I, II, III & IV
BRED BY THE SLUMS I, II, III
BLAST FOR ME I & II
ROTTEN TO THE CORE I II III
A BRONX TALE I, II, III
DUFFLE BAG CARTEL I II III IV V VI
HEARTLESS GOON I II III IV V
A SAVAGE DOPEBOY I II
DRUG LORDS I II III
CUTTHROAT MAFIA I II
KING OF THE TRENCHES
By **Ghost**

LAY IT DOWN I & II
LAST OF A DYING BREED I II
BLOOD STAINS OF A SHOTTA I & II III
By **Jamaica**

LOYAL TO THE GAME I II III
LIFE OF SIN I, II III
By **TJ & Jelissa**

IF LOVING HIM IS WRONG…I & II
LOVE ME EVEN WHEN IT HURTS I II III
By **Jelissa**

PUSH IT TO THE LIMIT
By **Bre' Hayes**

BLOOD AND MAYHEM | JJ DORSEY

BLOODY COMMAS I & II
SKI MASK CARTEL I, II & III
KING OF NEW YORK I II, III IV V
RISE TO POWER I II III
COKE KINGS I II III IV V
BORN HEARTLESS I II III IV
KING OF THE TRAP I II
By **T.J. Edwards**

WHEN THE STREETS CLAP BACK I & II III
THE HEART OF A SAVAGE I II III IV
MONEY MAFIA I II
LOYAL TO THE SOIL I II III
By **Jibril Williams**

A DISTINGUISHED THUG STOLE MY HEART I II & III
LOVE SHOULDN'T HURT I II III IV
RENEGADE BOYS 1-4
PAID IN KARMA 1-3
SAVAGE STORMS 1-3
AN UNFORESEEN LOVE 1-3
BABY, I'M WINTERTIME COLD 1-3
A THUG'S STREET PRINCESS 1&2
By **Meesha**

A GANGSTER'S CODE 1-3
A GANGSTER'S SYN 1-3
THE SAVAGE LIFE 1-3
CHAINED TO THE STREETS 1-3
BLOOD ON THE MONEY 1-3
A GANGSTA'S PAIN 1-3
BEAUTIFUL LIES AND UGLY TRUTHS
CHURCH IN THESE STREETS
By **J-Blunt**

CUM FOR ME 1-8
An LDP Erotica Collaboration

BLOOD OF A BOSS 1-5
SHADOWS OF THE GAME
TRAP BASTARD
By **Askari**

THE STREETS BLEED MURDER 1-3
THE HEART OF A GANGSTA 1-3
By **Jerry Jackson**

WHEN A GOOD GIRL GOES BAD
By **Adrienne**

THE COST OF LOYALTY 1-3
By **Kweli**

BRIDE OF A HUSTLA 1-3
THE FETTI GIRLS 1-3
CORRUPTED BY A GANGSTA 1-4
BLINDED BY HIS LOVE
THE PRICE YOU PAY FOR LOVE 1-3
DOPE GIRL MAGIC 1-3
By **Destiny Skai**

A KINGPIN'S AMBITION
A KINGPIN'S AMBITION II
I MURDER FOR THE DOUGH
By **Ambitious**

TRUE SAVAGE 1-7
DOPE BOY MAGIC 1-3
MIDNIGHT CARTEL 1-3
CITY OF KINGZ 1&2
NIGHTMARE ON SILENT AVE
THE PLUG OF LIL MEXICO 1&2
CLASSIC CITY
By **Chris Green**

A GANGSTER'S REVENGE 1-4
THE BOSS MAN'S DAUGHTERS 1-5
A SAVAGE LOVE 1&2
BAE BELONGS TO ME 1&2
A HUSTLER'S DECEIT 1-3
WHAT BAD BITCHES DO 1-3
SOUL OF A MONSTER 1-3
KILL ZONE
A DOPE BOY'S QUEEN 1-3
TIL DEATH 1-3
IMMA DIE BOUT MINE 1-6
DYING FOR LIKES
By **Aryanna**

A DOPEBOY'S PRAYER
By **Eddie "Wolf" Lee**

THE KING CARTEL 1-3
By **Frank Gresham**

THESE NIGGAS AIN'T LOYAL 1-3
By **Nikki Tee**

GANGSTA SHYT 1-3
By **CATO**

THE ULTIMATE BETRAYAL
By **Phoenix**

BOSS'N UP 1-3
By **Royal Nicole**

I LOVE YOU TO DEATH
By **Destiny J**

I RIDE FOR MY HITTA
I STILL RIDE FOR MY HITTA
By **Misty Holt**

LOVE & CHASIN' PAPER
By **Qay Crockett**

TO DIE IN VAIN
SINS OF A HUSTLA
By **ASAD**

BROOKLYN HUSTLAZ
By **Boogsy Morina**

BROOKLYN ON LOCK 1 & 2
By **Sonovia**

GANGSTA CITY
By **Teddy Duke**

A DRUG KING AND HIS DIAMOND 1-3
A DOPEMAN'S RICHES
HER MAN, MINE'S TOO 1&2
CASH MONEY HO'S
THE WIFEY I USED TO BE 1&2
PRETTY GIRLS DO NASTY THINGS
By **Nicole Goosby**

LIPSTICK KILLAH 1-3
CRIME OF PASSION 1-3
FRIEND OR FOE 1-3
By **Mimi**

TRAPHOUSE KING 1-3
KINGPIN KILLAZ 1-3
STREET KINGS 1&2
PAID IN BLOOD 1&2
CARTEL KILLAZ 1-3
DOPE GODS 1&2
By **Hood Rich**

THE STREETS ARE CALLING
By **Duquie Wilson**

STEADY MOBBN' 1-3
THE STREETS STAINED MY SOUL 1-3
By **Marcellus Allen**

WHO SHOT YA 1-3
SON OF A DOPE FIEND 1-4
HEAVEN GOT A GHETTO 1&2
SKI MASK MONEY 1&2
By **Renta**

GORILLAZ IN THE BAY 1-4
TEARS OF A GANGSTA 1/&2
3X KRAZY 1&2
STRAIGHT BEAST MODE 1&2
By **DE'KARI**

TRIGGADALE 1-3
MURDA WAS THE CASE 1-3
By **Elijah R. Freeman**

SLAUGHTER GANG 1-3
RUTHLESS HEART 1-3
By **Willie Slaughter**

GOD BLESS THE TRAPPERS 1-3
THESE SCANDALOUS STREETS 1-3
FEAR MY GANGSTA 1-5
THESE STREETS DON'T LOVE NOBODY 1-2
BURY ME A G 1-5
A GANGSTA'S EMPIRE 1-4
THE DOPEMAN'S BODYGAURD 1&2
THE REALEST KILLAZ 1-3
THE LAST OF THE OGS 1-3
By **Tranay Adams**

MARRIED TO A BOSS 1-3
By **Destiny Skai & Chris Green**

KINGZ OF THE GAME 1-7
CRIME BOSS 1-4
By **Playa Ray**

FUK SHYT
By **Blakk Diamond**

DON'T F#CK WITH MY HEART 1&2
By **Linnea**

ADDICTED TO THE DRAMA 1-3
IN THE ARM OF HIS BOSS
By **Jamila**

LOYALTY AIN'T PROMISED 1&2
By **Keith Williams**

YAYO 1-4
A SHOOTER'S AMBITION 1&2
BRED IN THE GAME
By **S. Allen**

TRAP GOD 1-3
RICH $AVAGE 1-3
MONEY IN THE GRAVE 1-3
CARTEL MONEY 1&2
By **Martell Troublesome Bolden**

FOREVER GANGSTA 1&2
GLOCKS ON SATIN SHEETS 1&2
By **Adrian Dulan**

TOE TAGZ 1-4
LEVELS TO THIS SHYT 1&2
IT'S JUST ME AND YOU
By **Ah'Million**

KINGPIN DREAMS 1-3
RAN OFF ON DA PLUG
By **Paper Boi Rari**

THE STREETS MADE ME 1-3
By **Larry D. Wright**

CONFESSIONS OF A GANGSTA 1-4
CONFESSIONS OF A JACKBOY 1-3
CONFESSIONS OF A HITMAN
CONFESSIONS OF A DOPE BOY
By **Nicholas Lock**

I'M NOTHING WITHOUT HIS LOVE
SINS OF A THUG
TO THE THUG I LOVED BEFORE
A GANGSTA SAVED XMAS
IN A HUSTLER I TRUST
By **Monet Dragun**

QUIET MONEY 1-3
THUG LIFE 1-3
EXTENDED CLIP 1&2
A GANGSTA'S PARADISE
By **Trai'Quan**

CAUGHT UP IN THE LIFE 1-3
THE STREETS NEVER LET GO 1-3
By **Robert Baptiste**

NEW TO THE GAME 1-3
MONEY, MURDER & MEMORIES 1-3
By **Malik D. Rice**

CREAM 2-3
THE STREETS WILL TALK
By **Yolanda Moore**

THE STREETS WILL NEVER CLOSE 1-3
By **K'ajji**

LIFE OF A SAVAGE 1-4
A GANGSTA'S QUR'AN 1-4
MURDA SEASON 1-3
GANGLAND CARTEL 1-3
CHI'RAQ GANGSTAS 1-4
KILLERS ON ELM STREET 1-3
JACK BOYZ N DA BRONX 1-3
A DOPEBOY'S DREAM 1-3
JACK BOYS VS DOPE BOYS 1-3
COKE GIRLZ
COKE BOYS
SOSA GANG 1&2
BRONX SAVAGES
BODYMORE KINGPINS
BLOOD OF A GOON
By **Romell Tukes**

CONCRETE KILLA 1-3
VICIOUS LOYALTY 1-3
BLOODY MONEY BAGS
By **Kingpen**

THE ULTIMATE SACRIFICE 1-6
KHADIFI
IF YOU CROSS ME ONCE 1-3
ANGEL 1-4
IN THE BLINK OF AN EYE
By **Anthony Fields**

THE LIFE OF A HOOD STAR
By **Ca$h & Rashia Wilson**

NIGHTMARES OF A HUSTLA 1-3
BLOOD AND GAMES 1&2
By **King Dream**

GHOST MOB
By **Stilloan Robinson**

HARD AND RUTHLESS 1&2
MOB TOWN 251
THE BILLIONAIRE BENTLEYS 1-3
REAL G'S MOVE IN SILENCE
By **Von Diesel**

MOB TIES 1-7
SOUL OF A HUSTLER, HEART OF A KILLER 1-3
GORILLAZ IN THE TRENCHES
OOPS CRY TOO 1&2
THE DAUGHTER OF A CARTEL BOSS
By **SayNoMore**

BODYMORE MURDERLAND 1-3
THE BIRTH OF A GANGSTER 1-4
By **Delmont Player**

FOR THE LOVE OF A BOSS 1&2
By **C. D. Blue**

KILLA KOUNTY 1-5
TENDER
By **Khufu**

MOBBED UP 1-4
THE BRICK MAN 1-5
THE COCAINE PRINCESS 1-10
STEPPERS 1-3
SUPER GREMLIN 1-4
A GANGSTA'S SON
By **King Rio**

MONEY GAME 1&2
By **Smoove Dolla**

A GANGSTA'S KARMA 1-5
By **FLAME**

KING OF THE TRENCHES 1-3
By **GHOST & TRANAY ADAMS**

BAD BITCHES WIT GUNZ 1&2
PROBLEM SOLVED
By "Christopher Diesel" Hornezes

QUEEN OF THE ZOO 1&2
By **Black Migo**

GRIMEY WAYS 1-3
BETRAYAL OF A G
By **Ray Vinci**

XMAS WITH AN ATL SHOOTER
By **Ca$h & Destiny Skai**

KING KILLA 1&2
By **Vincent "Vitto" Holloway**

BETRAYAL OF A THUG 1&2
By **Fre$h**

COUNTDOWN OF A KILLA 1&2
SEX, MURDER AND GOD 1&2
GUNS DOWN, BOTTOMS UP 1&2
By Lo-Life

THE MURDER QUEENS 1-7
By **Michael Gallon**

FOR THE LOVE OF BLOOD 1-4
By **Jamel Mitchell**

BLOOD AND MAYHEM | JJ DORSEY

HOOD CONSIGLIERE 1&2
NO TIME FOR ERROR
By **Keese**

PROTÉGÉ OF A LEGEND 1,2&3
LOVE IN THE TRENCHES 1&2
By **Corey Robinson**

THE PLUG'S RUTHLESS DAUGHTER 1&2
By **Tony Daniels**

BORN IN THE GRAVE 1-3
CRIME PAYS
By **Self Made Tay**

MOAN IN MY MOUTH
By **XTASY**

TORN BETWEEN A GANGSTER AND A GENTLEMAN
By **J-BLUNT & Miss Kim**

LOYALTY IS EVERYTHING 1-3
CITY OF SMOKE 1-3
By **Molotti**

HERE TODAY GONE TOMORROW 1&2
By **Fly Rock**

WOMEN LIE MEN LIE 1-4
FIFTY SHADES OF SNOW 1-3
STACK BEFORE YOU SPLURGE
GIRLS FALL LIKE DOMINOES
NAÏVE TO THE STREETS
By **ROY MILLIGAN**

PILLOW PRINCESS
By **S. Hawkins**

THE BUTTERFLY MAFIA 1-3
SALUTE MY SAVAGERY 1&2
By **Fumiya Payne**

THE LANE 1&2
By Ken-Ken Spence

THE PUSSY TRAP 1-5
By **Nene Capri**

DIRTY DNA
By **Blaque**

SANCTIFIED AND HORNY
by **XTASY**

BOOKS BY LDP'S CEO, CA$H

TRUST IN NO MAN
TRUST IN NO MAN 2
TRUST IN NO MAN 3
BONDED BY BLOOD
SHORTY GOT A THUG
THUGS CRY
THUGS CRY 2
THUGS CRY 3
TRUST NO BITCH
TRUST NO BITCH 2
TRUST NO BITCH 3
TIL MY CASKET DROPS
RESTRAINING ORDER
RESTRAINING ORDER 2
IN LOVE WITH A CONVICT
LIFE OF A HOOD STAR
XMAS WITH AN ATL SHOOTER

www.ingramcontent.com/pod-product-compliance
Lightning Source LLC
LaVergne TN
LVHW010918110826
845149LV00013B/2411

* 9 7 8 1 9 7 1 7 7 0 1 5 4 *